Also by Saci Lloyd

The Carbon Diaries 2015
Shortlisted for the Costa Children's Book Award
The Carbon Diaries 2017
Momentum
Shortlisted for the Guardian Children's Book Award

SACI LLOYD

QUANTUM DROP

*Hodder
Children's
Books*

A division of Hachette Children's Books

For the 99%

I was born on the prairies where the wind blew free and there was nothing to break the light of the sun. I was born where there were no fences . . .

Geronimo

I guess what I'm going to tell you is kind of a love story, tho' if you met me face to face, you'd never in a million years take me for the romantic type. But when a girl like Tais comes into your life and turns it upside down, well, you've got to lay yourself out on the line, because otherwise what are you . . . some kind of dead man walking? Least that's the way I see it. But relax, I'm not going to give you my whole draggy backstory; me in nappies and all that *Momma din't give me enough love* and *Daddy was a rolling stone* crap . . . that's not where this is heading, no, not at all.

I suppose I've got to pick somewhere to begin, because y'know, it's not like all of the madness sprang up out of *nowhere*, but looking back on it now, the exam hall was

1

probably the first time the pressure blew the lid right off of me. So I'm going to start there. The final week of my college exams, in the area Test Hall, and it's a quarter past three in booth C for Candidate Number 3027. Anthony, Griffin. Oh, and look I'm going to level with you, that's not my real name. I picked it up online. But please don't take it personal, I don't mean to be rude or anything. I'm only faking up a name so it's clean between us. So that I don't know you and you don't know me because it's easier that way, easier to *talk*, right?

And so there I am, plugged into the testFrame, Biology: Paper 2 and in truth things ain't going so great for me. In fact, I'm kind of a mess. Twenty minutes have jagged past since the test began and I haven't even looked at the questions on the screen in front of me. Instead my eyes are blank-glued to the digital clock in the far right hand corner of the monitor like I'm some kind of zombie. But I'm no zombie, I'm a really smart guy. No really, I'm not bragging, I'm *smart*. Everybody says so. I'm up for a scholarship and everything.

And this exam is my big moment. It's my way to blast clear of the Debtbelt for ever. But I'm not doing what I'm supposed to do. I'm not scribbling down all that knowledge that I've spent endless months and years cramming into my skull. No, I'm blowing my future, big style, as I sit, motionless and hypnotised by the row of dials nestling alongside the digital clock, each one reading a separate bit of me: my heart rate, blood sugar, adrenaline levels . . . and all of the read-outs pounding away in the red zones. I'm amazed the principal hasn't called an ambulance; I mean, why hook all of us up to this shit if he doesn't mean to help us out when we fly off the scale?

And it's like I'm magnetised to the zigs and the zags and the motion of the dials. I can feel my left hand trembling, gripped tight around the exam pad as sweat trickles all the way down my arm from my back. True, it's a hot day and all, but I am way beyond hot. I'm oozing, slip-sliding sweat, a steady trickle dripping from my palms, drumming out a staccato . . .

ᵗuₙk ᵗuₙk

rhythm as it hits the pad; forming a dark stain that spreads across the cobalt-blue foam. I've got no focus, no mind, no breath. And that's when I start to think that there's no way to say time in numbers in the Micmac language. You just can't do it. For sure, there are words for day and night, sunrise, sunset, being young, or old, all that, but there's no word for an absolute time, like four o'clock, say, which is just this weird number we've made up to measure the world from outside itself.

And that's because for Native American Indians, time's all relative and if you want to make a meeting time, you have to say something *real* like, I'll see you when the sun falls behind those rocks . . . or when the shadows reach that wall. Something rooted in the physical world, you get me? Einstein stayed with the Indians once and said they were the best people to understand the law of relativity. Thinking this kind of shit in exams instead of answering questions is not cool, I do *know* that.

But trapped here in this place I can't find my focus. I'm floating above myself. I twist my neck, gaze around the room at all the kids, trapped inside their separate transparent cubicles, with their flushed faces and narrowed eyes, tongues poking out the corners of their mouths. You know the look. The *future generation*. All the different tribes of us. The winners, the losers, the geeks, the jokers, the sociopaths, the slackers. Homo habilis, Homo erectus, Homo neanderthalensis, Homo sapiens. Yeah, we're all here, all right. *Homo sapiens. Thinking human.* Jokes, right?

A girl across the way glances up, catches my roving eye and frowns at me. I make myself look back at my screen again. But it's no good. And I don't want to lie, it's all my fault; I haven't revised for even one minute. I haven't even set *foot* in college for weeks. A cold shiver runs across my flesh.

I see the ventilator. I hear the mechanical rasp as it pumps oxygen through the tube. I see her chest, strapped into a plastic guard as it rises and falls to the beat of the machine.

Man, this is a bad day for the whole big A Griffin future. But the thing is I just don't *want* it no more. I don't want to sell my brain for peanuts or laugh like a sad loser at my boss's sad loser jokes. That's what guys like me end up doing. And there are no jobs anyhow. No, if I had my way I'd step out of this exam hall and walk the earth like Grasshopper, yeah, fighting and fixing stuff and helping folks on my lonely trek to Nirvana. But I'm ashamed of my body, my soft hands. I don't know any knots, any nooses, any traps, any poisons, any anything that'd keep me alive. And that's what I want to be, a boy *alive*. I want it more'n anything in the world.

And I live where I live, right? In the Debtbelt. And from all I hear that's a lot of places nowadays. My name is Anthony Griffin and I *am* the boy next door. Nothing special 'bout me. I'm in every street in every neighbourhood and every city on earth. Hell, I probably live over the way from you . . . I'm in Athens and Baltimore and Berlin and

Buenos Aires and Detroit and Helsinki and Istanbul and Lisbon and Mexico City and Mumbai and Nairobi and Santiago and São Paulo and Shanghai and Stockholm and Tel Aviv and Tokyo and Toronto and Washington DC and wherever else you are. I'm global, man.

In the exam hall I close my eyes. I squeeze them shut against the images. But it's no good.

I see the tubes snaking into her ribcage. I see the liquid draining into a container at the foot of her bed. I watch the steady drip, drip as fluid is siphoned from her body, easing the pressure on her shattered chest.

And suddenly an ice-cold breaker of fear bubbles up in my chest, splashing bitter salt up through my throat, stinging my eyes, catching at my tongue. And as it surges upward, the wave passes out through the tip of my head, growing bigger and bigger until it towers above me, a wall of surging power. I crouch down in my seat, bracing myself for the impact. I've got to break free! If I stay here I'll drown. I've got to bust out before it's too late.

I hurl myself sideways just as the wave starts to crash. Flying across the aisle, I land in a sprawl into the cubicle opposite, my head connecting hard with someone's knee. I look up. Max. Of all the people to crunch my skull into

6

it has to be him. I hate that guy. He jerks his body backwards, his mouth twisting into a snarl. A shocked gasp echoes around the exam hall, as a thousand students turn around to stare.

My eyes lock on to Max's and for a long moment we stare at each other in mutual hatred.

'You, boy!'

The shout bounces off the hall walls. I turn my head. A man in a dark blue suit cut in the Asiamodern style is striding purposefully towards me. I look around wildly, trying to work out a plan. I can still fix this . . . pretend I fainted or something . . . that'd work, right? The man will be here any second. I order myself to do it, to do myself a favour for once in my miserable life. To smile at him, tell him I didn't eat breakfast . . . tell him I feel sick, beg for a second chance.

And for a second I lie on the floor, caught between two lines of action. The man is approaching fast, he stretches out his arm, reaching for me . . . and that's when I decide. Lurching to my feet, I set off full tilt for the exit, the hall blurring around me as I streak across the floor, reaching the ID barriers and smashing through them in one giant leap.

You should see me fly; I swear there's sparks flying off of my sneakers as I skid like a maniac down the corridors.

I don't stop till I bust out of the front gates of the exam centre and I don't stop even then, but keep on running, till my last breath is blown and I pull up at the crossroads on the High Street, fighting for air like a crazy fish on a line. For a moment I think I'm going to black out. I double up, beating down the nausea inside, but after a few minutes it starts to pass and I feel better, calmer. I'm not frightened any more. I spit a couple times and then straighten up.

I look around me in wonder, as if it's the first time I've ever been in this area. Why did I run here? I frown, trying to work out what day it is. I glance at my deck. Thursday. Yeah, of course. The day of my big exam. But that's all behind me now. A snapshot of the rota I've pinned up on my bedroom wall flashes into my mind. Thursday is Estate day. And the Estate is just over the way. That's why I'm here. Ah yeah, it all makes sense now.

But before I set off, I scan three-sixty, checking for any Betta boys on the prowl. I've got to take care. It's a scary time for me now, I don't mind telling you. My security levels are sky high. Not that they've ever been low since the crash. For years now I've taped credits to the base of my shoe and stuffed anything worth anything down my boxers *and* worn two pairs, the inside ones tight, tight. I've been robbed so many times it's not even funny. But things have been on a whole new level recently.

To my relief the street is clear, so I turn to the left, setting off at a good pace past the discount stores, fried chicken shops, bars and gambling joints. And as I walk by, again and again and again they roll past me, like they're on a repeating loop, like cheap background in a low-budget game. Dead-end stores on a busted street, lidded by dirty grey graffitied rollers. And me the superhero walking on by. But I ain't no hero, I'm just me and I jam my hands into my pockets and keep my head low, eyes down.

In a few minutes I reach Bobby's discount liquor store and, ducking around the side, I slip through a rusty gate into a dustbowl park that stretches, dry, towards the old canal. I pass through a line of trees and as I come out the other side, that's when I get my first view of the Estate; the north side of the tower block rising up like a rotten tooth. My grandad says a bank on the other side of the world owns half of all the apartments here. He says he bets they wish to high hell they didn't. Looks like we lost a war.

Skirting round some wiggy roses I break into a jog but when I reach the locked gates on the far side of the park, I pull up for a minute and again scan three-sixty, but mostly focusing on the strip of road that separates me from the great grey hulk of the Estate. All clear again.

Good. Grasping the topmost rail with my right hand, I hurdle over the gate, dart across the road, and on the far side I bounce on to the sidewalk and immediately cut sharp left, squeezing my body through a junk-filled side alley, before emerging a few seconds later in the central square of the Estate.

Pressed against the concrete, I blow out a breath and glance up at the great grey walls rising above me. It's like I've just broken into jail. But I can't stay here, I've got to get a move on. Skirting past a strip of broken-bottle-studded grass, I race through a playground area with a couple tyres hanging from rusty chains, and just a few paces beyond it I finally reach my destination; a raggedy corner of the parking lot, filled with scrap metal and broken pallets.

Flinging myself on the cracked asphalt behind a burnt-out car, I press myself flat. My friend Ali showed me this spot once, back when we still hung out together . . . and now it's *my* hiding place, my observation point. It smells like bitter weeds and vomit. It smells like whole lives gone up in smoke. But I don't care. I'm on a mission. I'm searching for a voice. The voice that's burnt right through me like a brand.

Lifting my head, I peer out from behind the blackened rear wheel arch of the car. This fried-up old boneshaker has two good observation points. The first is up front, a crawlspace where you can jam yourself behind the steering wheel on the melted front seat. From here you get a good view of the front wall of the Estate, all the way up to a fork in the zigzagging concrete walkways where the balcony widens, and people hang out together. If it's a warm day a lot of folk stop to chat there, mostly moms resting between flights with bags of shopping or maybe some frail old guys shooting the breeze. Sometimes you see them laugh and throw their heads back, leaning their elbows against the railings, but then you look at their arms and they're so frail and wispy, like little sparrow bones, like a puff of

11

wind would lift their whole bodies up, up, up and away.

It's funny but I used to like looking at the people up on the walkway, like I was some mad anthropologist watching all their ways without them knowing I was there. But I ain't got time for that now. My business today is with the far side of the parking lot. That's why I'm in the *second* observation point, down on the pavement behind the car. Because from here I can see right across the rutted asphalt, to where a gang of Betta are hanging out. I don't know if *he* is with them, I don't have a single clue to go on 'cept the message he left on Tais' voicemail, the message I overheard in her bedroom the night before, the sound of his voice, rough like sandpaper, telling her to meet him on the fifth floor, apartment 13 at three thirty. That's all I've got to go on.

I crawl as far forward as I can through a line of weeds until my shoulder is hard up against the front wheel arch. I'm straining to hear what the Betta boys are saying but I'm too far away to catch actual words. Still I can pick up tones, the sound of their voices for sure, and that's a start.

There are four of them over there right now, bunched in a loose knot around an entryway. The Betta *splendens*, the fighting fish. Four slim, dark figures with bleached-out Mohawks, flashes of green and pink jagging up through the peroxide. One boy, a little bigger than all the rest, is facing in my direction. He perches on a bike rail, eyes hooded, his knee jigging a jerky tattoo under his crimson trench coat. Suddenly he lifts his head, looks directly at me, and his mouth twists in a crooked smile. I fall flat against the earth like a bullet's knocked me down and I lay there, squirming against the ground, praying he hasn't seen me. Because believe me, spying on the Betta ain't an option, not on the Estate. They *own* this place.

Suddenly I freeze. Hot, stinking breath on my cheek. Hardly daring to breathe, I force my neck to turn, to gaze upward into the bulging face of the dog, his ears razored down into scarred stubs. Now I understand the Betta's twisted grin. He spotted me for sure and sent his dog to pin me down. It's an old Betta trick. I flick my gaze back over to the far side of the lot. The boy is standing now, searching for us, but the wheel arch is blocking his view. Putting his fingers in his mouth, he lets fly with a high, shrill whistle. The dog's head lifts and he takes a pace forward, seeking out his master.

I don't need a second chance.

Springing up, I launch myself over the car, scrabbling over the rotting metal, before I land, hard, and break into a mad lunge across the lot, scattering a bunch of little kids as I cut between two parked cars. One of them screams after me in Urdu. Aiming for a stairwell, I cut to the right and race up a flight of plankboard stairs. Behind me I can hear the dog's paws shredding the wood as he closes in. I put on a last desperate burst of speed. I've got to get somewhere high, and fast! Suddenly a door opens up ahead. A Betta girl in a ripped silver T-shirt stands in the entrance, she smiles . . .

Slowly the world comes back into focus. I'm sprawled out on the floor, lying perfectly still, staring at the after-image of a curved line of light that flickers over my vision. Concrete presses cold against my ripped skin, the dog's jaws are at my throat. The girl must've tripped me somehow. I turn my head slightly, the Betta boy is now standing over me. He leans forward and his crimson coat falls open, revealing a long, sleek blade strapped to his chest. I gaze up into his face. How old is he? Fifteen; sixteen, max. Grinning, he releases the blade from its sheath and I watch, mesmerised, as it dips towards my throat.

And then a voice comes from the shadows. 'No!'

A flicker of irritation crosses the boy's smooth forehead, but his hand stills.

'Not your business, man. *Mine*,' he mutters.

I hear soft footsteps approach, and then an oxblood twelve-hole boot appears in my field of vision, its steel-tipped toe tapping once, delicately, against the boy's chest. The dog suddenly whimpers, backs away.

'I said *no*.'

I stare up into the Betta boy's face, scarcely daring to breathe. He rocks back on his heels and, for a long moment, sits hunched over me, the folds of his jacket falling around him like vulture feathers.

He glances up, jerks his head. 'Cost yer.'

'How much?'

'Ten on the credit.'

'Too much. Five.'

The boy sucks his teeth. 'Five ain't worth letting him live. It's ten or I cut and be damned. You ain't all that, Ali.'

A leather-gloved hand comes into sight, taps the side of the boy's skull.

'You want to chance it? I give you five for the runt and that's my trade.'

Slowly the boy slots his knife back into its sheath, his face flat with displeasure, but as he bends I see a gleam of triumph briefly flash in his eyes. *He's got what he wanted*.

'Then call Filipino Johnny to witness.'

'Ai'ght.'

The boy pushes up from me like I'm a piece of meat, but I daren't move, not yet. Not till the deal is done. I know the drill. After a minute there comes the slow, dragging sound of limping footsteps on the plank boards. Rolling my head sideways, I catch a glimpse of a middle-aged man in a dark jacket, his oily ponytail falling over the fabric. As he gets closer, he dips a dirty-fingered hand into his pocket, pulling out a scratched and battered kalculus.

'Trade!' he cries as he steps into the stairwell.

For a moment I am left alone, flat on the ground, as the three figures huddle together. I see a flicker of credit changing hands and then suddenly the Betta boy turns and strides over to me. Bending down swiftly, his face centimetres from mine, he lifts an amused eyebrow, causing the long, steel bolt drilled into the bone above his eye socket to slant across his forehead like a scar.

'Din't mean nothing by it, Younger. Market slow these past days. When I see you down in the lot there I reckoned I'd take a chance on Ali comin' through with some hard credit, seeing how's you two go back a ways.'

And then he sticks out a hand. My throat tightens, but I've got no choice but to take it. As his hand slides into mine, it feels like a velvet glove, like he's never done nothing but sneaky, slimy work his whole life. But I have to shake. It shows I understand it ain't personal when I get jacked or ripped off. It shows I understand it's just business. Even if all I want to do is rip his throat out.

And you've got to keep sweet with the Betta because they are the power. They're the only ones to turn to, if you

16

don't want to disappear off the grid. Banks stopped lending to ordinary folk long ago and there's no safety net no more. You go on the waiting list to get assistance, Government puts you on a wait list a year and a half long. So if you're making five hundred a month with two kids to feed . . . what are you gonna do? You go to the Betta, or at least that's what you do in this city. The Betta they jack you some dirty credit, they get you through the week. But you take the money, you pay the price, all right. The Betta be the bank and the judge and the feds rolled into one and you'd best be ready to pay come collection day.

The Betta boy rises and he and Filipino Johnny slink away into the shadows, the dog pulling a rolling trot by their side. I let out a long breath and slowly pull myself to my knees.

'Did he hurt you?'

Finally I turn to look up at him. Dark skin, strong jaw, scar cutting across his full lower lip, twisting the skin a lighter shade of shiny pink where it catches. *Ali*.

I rub my head. 'No, man. More like a massage.'

His eyes spark with laughter. 'Shiatsu?'

'The works. Threw me in a complimentary head rub an' all.' I wipe at a trickle of blood running down my cheek.

The laugh dies from his face as quick as it came.

'What you doing down here, Anthony? You know this place is off limits . . .'

I frown. 'I go where I want.'

His eyes narrow. 'I only just got to you in time. He would've stuck you.'

'No, he wouldn't. He was using me as bait . . . y'know . . . because you and me got history. I'll pay you back.'

Ali runs his fingers through his sculpted black quiff. 'Don't want your money . . . But man, you can't come here no more. I can't be seen to be looking out after no one . . . I've just made captain.'

'I wasn't looking for you . . .'

'What then?'

'My business.'

Ali suddenly puts out a hand, grabs me by the arm. 'No, Anthony. You ain't got no business here. This place is dead to you.'

We stare at each other a long moment. There's too much to say so we don't say anything. You know how that is? Ali's fingers tighten on my flesh. 'I don't know what I'd do if anything happened to you or Lola. You got to promise me to keep 'way.'

Our eyes meet and it's us again, for a second. And then the moment's gone. Ali straightens, and, without another word, he turns on his heel and walks away.

Balancing on the balls of my toes, I listen to the fading sound of his boots on the plankboard steps, and suddenly my mind flies back to the day we first met – the day of my first ever fight. After the first time it gets easier, I guess, but the first fight is so hard; you're trembling and your legs are shaking and you don't know if you can even stand up. It was with my mate, Beat. I don't even know how it started, but I do remember I'd just gotten dumped. I had this little girlfriend, Amy, and she skipped out at break time and finished with me, *bam*. Brutal, right in front of a whole crowd she did it. And I don't know how that turned into me and Beat fighting but it did, out in the school yard.

And when a fight starts you black out, right? All I can really remember now is tears and a ripped shirt and swinging Beat and getting nowhere. But I don't remember any pain. I mean, it felt like my head was gonna fall off, it felt so *big*. But it didn't *hurt*.

And that's when I met Ali. It was his first day in school and he was out in the yard watching us. As soon as we were done, he walked over and grinned at me. And that was it, we were tight right from that moment. Cos he saw me, that I was fighting for real. And that's when things got good for me. I mean, I was *ready* to fight now, but I didn't

19

need to any more. Nobody messed with Ali.

He was a foster kid. Not that anyone knew then, he only told me later when we got really close. And what a story he had. When he was six years old he started getting beats with a baseball bat, and it took three long years of this before the feds came and took him off his mom, so he was knocked about for all those years, right, without anyone looking out for him. And by the time he came to my school he'd been through like five different care homes, he told me they ain't like they are on the tube; he got battered in there too. In the last one, before he came to live near me, Ali got so mad he smashed his own head in with a pay phone.

So even by the time we met he'd been fighting his whole life. But man, did he hate bullies. It wound him up so bad when smaller kids got picked on. I don't know what it was – maybe he'd been through so much he couldn't stand to watch someone else getting hurt.

But that's all in the past because Ali's turned Betta now and he's rising thru' the ranks fast.

It's like I never knew him at all.

I slowly lever myself up from the floor, and as I rise, such a wave of longing hits me – for the past, for *how things used to be*. It hurts more'n a Betta fist, I can tell you. I stagger sideways from the impact. I need to be with someone close, someone who really knows me, from before, y'know? And right now that can only mean one person – it's got to be Lola.

I run my hands over my body. My neck and head are sore as all hell, but apart from that I'm OK, 'cept from my left side where I fell. But even as I stretch out my stiff thigh, I know I'm lucky. Who knows how far the boy would've gone if Ali hadn't showed. A spark of anger lights in my chest. *Ali, the big hero*. I turn, and taking the plankboard steps fast, I re-emerge on the Estate parking lot and set off at a limping trot for Lola's place.

Some fifteen minutes of intricate back-route weaving later, I reach her condo block, and slipping inside the elevator, I ride it up to the twenty-second floor. After a brief pause, the doors slide open on a marble walkway and at first glance you might think this place is pretty fancy, but if you look a little closer you'll see there's paint peeling and chunks of plaster missing all over the show. I mean, compared to other places they sure do a pretty good job of covering over the cracks in this condo, but the cracks are there all right, and everyone's family is kind of like Lola's family. Only her dad working part time and her married brother just moved back in with his wife and kid.

Arriving at her front door I press the buzzer. As I wait, I give my face a quick wipe, in case there's any blood spatters showing, because Mrs Rossi, well, I don't know how she'd take to a blood-spattered boy on her doorstep. But I needn't have bothered because it's Lola's brother, Jon, who swings the door open, beer bottle in hand, and he wouldn't care if I rocked up with *no* head. He's kind of a bitter guy, but I don't blame him; I mean, *I'd* be bitter if my baby was as badass ugly as his.

I try a smile. 'Oh, hi . . . Is Lola here?'

'Maybe.' He glowers at me from the front step, making no move to let me past.

'Oh.'

But then comes Mrs Rossi's voice from inside. 'Is that you, Anthony?'

I lift my head. 'Yeah.'

'Well, come on in, boy.'

I slide inside, under the heavy gaze of Jon. And I'm so happy because Lola's place feels more like home than mine does, you know how that is? Ever since my mom started working two jobs and the nightshift I'm lucky to see her more'n a couple hours a week. Stepping into the hallway I take a couple paces along the corridor before stepping into the living room. A dumb talent immersive blares from the tube and I peer over Mrs Rossi's shoulder as a blonde girl struts into view, her onscreen head twice the size of ours.

Mrs Rossi shakes her head disapprovingly.

'Bloody actress.'

I grin. 'You don't like her, Mrs R?'

She twists in her chair, her tiny dog peering out at me from under her arm. 'No I do not. Trollop.' She waves her arm towards the other contestants, waiting in the wings.

'It's JJ I want to win.'

The camera pans to a pale boy with raven wisps.

'Ah, there he is now!' sighs Mrs Rossi.

I rest my arms on the back of the sofa. 'Why him?'

'He's got a rare blood disorder, poor little lamb.'

I point to another kid, dressed in a white jumpsuit. 'What about him, tho'? He looks like he could use a win.'

Lola's mom tuts in disgust. 'Him? He's gotten a criminal record for waving a gun in the school canteen. He'll shoot the bleedin' contestants up if he thought it'd get him through to the next round.' She suddenly looks up into my face. 'You feeling all right? You look awful pale.'

'I'm good.'

She sighs. *I'm good*. And what's that supposed to mean? You kids.' But her eyes are kind and she reaches out, pats me on the hand. 'Go on up, Anthony . . . but be careful if she's working. She told me she might have caught a trade.' Her eyes slide towards Jon in the corner. 'Makes one of us, right?'

Running upstairs, I stop on the landing and knock on Lola's bedroom door. No answer. I chew my lip. Normally I'd never bug her if I knew she was working, but I'm so past normal after the day I've just had . . . I've got to see her, even if it's for a couple minutes. After a few seconds I gently push her door open.

Lola sits cross-legged on her bed, plugged into the Drop, her eyes a soft grey blank behind her visor as she leans against the bedroom wall. Damn, she *is* working. I crouch in front of her, wave my hand, but she doesn't

24

even blink. She must be in pretty deep. I daren't touch her; it's a killer to pull someone from the outside, 'specially the level Lola works at. I tap my teeth, unsure. I hate the Drop, but I hate the way I feel right now even more. I've got to go in. Just for five minutes. Then I'll be on my way.

I glance around the room, searching for a visor. Lola always has a couple spares around. Digging under a pile of discs on the floor, I catch a flash of silver and I pull the visor out. It's last year's model, but it'll do. Reaching over to her deck, I activate a new channel and then I sit down next to Lola on the bed, slip the 'trodes on to my temples, slide the visor over my eyes and jack in.

Immediately the room begins to rotate, faster and faster until it becomes a moving sphere, flowering outwards along an expanding axis that sweeps me along Lola's trail . . . until suddenly I'm standing at a traffic-choked intersection under a cobalt-blue sky, the ferocious sun beating down on the cars, taxis, limousines and scooters that flash by. Shielding my eyes, I look around the cityscape, trying to work out where I am inside the Drop.

Craning my neck I can just make out some street signs angled high on a pole. I'm at the junction of Rio Branco and Vitoria, whatever that means. A couple of office workers drift by, I catch a snatch of conversation . . .

maybe Spanish, Portuguese? I turn. Behind me a plush, five star high-rise hotel towers above the street. Above the entrance a green flag with a yellow diamond enclosing a blue globe flaps lazily in the heavy air. I frown. That's the Brazilian flag, right? So this must be São Paulo, the new money capital of America. But where's Lola?

Suddenly I feel a new tightening sensation at my temples and the street blurs as I start to move again, but in seconds my vision refocuses once more and now I'm standing in a suite on the ground floor of the hotel. I'm on the inside now.

I turn, scanning the room. Lola *must* be here somewhere . . . and then I see her. She's only a couple of metres away, sitting in a relaxed curve at a bank of monitors in front of a heavy, framed oil painting, her face a smooth mask of concentration as she works her deck. And then she looks up, her kohl-rimmed eyes widening with surprise as she sees me. I wave. She hesitates then waves back, a fast flicker of her delicate fingers. Grinning, I stride over to her side.

'What's up, Lola?'

She frowns. 'What are you doing here?'

My smile fades. 'Good to see you too.'

Lola's face softens slightly. 'I'm *working*, man.'

'Who for?'

26

She gestures towards a small curved bar set at the far end of the suite.

'Him.'

I turn. A heavy-set businessman sits slumped on a high stool, one impossibly shined-up shoe resting against the metal rail that circles the base of the bar.

'Handsome.'

'Don't be a jerk. First job I've caught in weeks.'

I straighten. She ain't going to talk to me if I act like a jerk.

'So what're you buying for him?'

She shakes her head. 'Selling, Anthony. I'm shorting Florida orange juice.'

'What's that mean?'

'You really want to know?'

'Yeah.'

Lola beckons me over to her monitor. 'I'm basically betting the market will go down. Shares in Florida Citrus Ltd are currently trading at 1.57 credits . . . but I figure they'll drop as low as .45 by tomorrow.'

I jerk my thumb over my shoulder. 'He brought you in here to *buy* orange juice shares? That's a bit lame isn't it?'

She shakes her head sadly, as if it's unbelievable someone can be so slow. 'No. He doesn't have to *buy* to bet. He's allowing me to take a position for him on whether the market is going to go up or down.'

I narrow my eyes. 'And that's legal?'

'Yes, totally. Apart from me being underage to trade. But I've got that covered. Fake ID.'

'But why orange juice?'

Her eyes glint. 'Well that's how come I got this gig. I've been researching this for weeks. My guess is Hurricane Theresa is going to sweep back in over Florida and wipe out the orange harvest in the southern part of the state.'

'And is it?'

'I think so. The national weather says Theresa will pass Florida and go out to sea, but I've got a live storm feed rolling and I've tracked Theresa's every move for ten days. I'm almost definite she's heading back to shore. And when that happens the price of Florida Citrus Ltd is going to collapse. And that's when I make my man a killing.'

I shake my head. 'When do you get time to work all this out?'

Lola rubs absently at the smear of iridescent turquoise sweeping across her eyelid. 'Got to. No way I'm going to fund uni otherwise, right?'

She suddenly looks me full in the face. 'You look terrible. You getting any sleep, Anthony?'

'Cheers. I just got robbed . . . That's why I swung by really . . .'

Lola flings her hand up. 'Damn. What you let me go on about OJ for?'

I shrug.

'Where were you?' she asks.

'The Estate.'

Her lips thin. 'Well, you had it coming then. Lucky you din't get cut.'

'Nearly did. Ali paid me out.'

Her face closes off completely. 'You should be flattered he even remembers your name.'

I sigh. Maybe coming to see Lola was a bad idea. *Time heals all things* is some proper BS, right? Lola's still in love with Ali, you can see it raw in her face. But he might as well be dead as far as she's concerned. The day he turned Betta she never spoke to him again. Not one word. One year and counting. Lola Rossi is *hardcore*.

She frowns. 'What were you doing at the Estate anyway?'

I shrug. 'Just hanging out . . . looking.'

'For what?'

'Nothing.' I stare out the window.

I can't tell her about the voice. No one can know how much of a coward I've been. A flash of movement from the street outside catches my eye. A sleek, matt-black sedan is pulling up at the front of the hotel and as I watch,

29

a bodyguard jumps out, an ugly beast in a dark suit. He scans the street and then gestures an all-clear for the occupant of the car. I catch a brief glimpse of a bald-headed man emerging from the interior and for a moment, I find myself wondering who he is in reality . . . I mean, who gets to cruise around a high level of the Drop like that?

'Anthony?' Lola taps me on the arm.

I blink and suddenly the wave catches me again, the great curl of longing . . . for the smell of Tais, the feel of her warm skin, for how the ragged chip in her right front tooth feels under my tongue. I bite back the pain. This was a stupid idea coming here, as if being with Lola could fix *that*.

I glare at her.

'How do you do it?'

'What?'

'Move on so easy.' My voice turns suddenly savage. 'It's like she meant nothing to you.'

A red spot appears on Lola's high cheekbones, but she keeps her voice level. 'That's low. Even for you—'

A shout comes from the far side of the room.

'Menina, vem aqui!'

We turn together. Lola's boss has been joined at the bar by the bodyguard, the one I was just watching outside.

What's he doing here? The businessman waves his hand, urgently gesturing to Lola.

Lola frowns. 'Now what?' She picks up her jacket, smoothes her hair. '*Estou chegando*, sir.'

But for some reason the bodyguard is pointing at me.

Lola nudges me. 'You know that guy?'

'No.'

'Then why's he jabbing his finger towards you?'

'Don't know.'

'You sure?'

I shake my head. 'Never seen him in my life.'

The bodyguard starts to walk towards us. He reaches inside his jacket. I catch a gleam of metal and suddenly Lola pushes me hard in the chest.

'He's a Drop fed. Jump out, Anthony!'

I reach for my visor, but as I fumble to hit the decompression button, the guard breaks into a run, heading straight towards me. There's no way I'm gonna make the jump in time.

'Run!' Lola shouts.

I whirl around, my sneakers squealing on the polished floor as I head for the foyer. Reaching the door in seconds, I charge flat out through the reception area, but I can feel the guy gaining on me. As I dodge the front desk, he makes a grab for my arm and I leap sideways, crashing into a palm – I stagger – and then suddenly the hotel walls begin to warp and curve, the paintings sloping away from me in a series of impossible angles. I desperately try to keep upright – but the floor is collapsing beneath me. My outstretched foot catches the corner of a Persian rug and suddenly I'm falling, tumbling into a dark hole where the rug lay only seconds before.

Landing heavily on a sticky hallway carpet I lie still, stunned. I stare around me. The old hotel has completely vanished, but it's weird, right, because I'm *still* in a hotel, but it's like I've dropped four stars over the course of the jump. This place is a dump. Rising to my feet, I flatten myself against a chipboard wall as a couple bustles past, the guy dragging an oversized suitcase behind him. And then suddenly the door directly in front of me flies open and the bodyguard appears, squeezing himself into the corridor alongside me.

Before I can react, he grabs me by the arm. 'What're you running for, boy?'

I stare up into his great jowly face.

He tightens his grip. 'Answer me!'

I swallow. 'Nothing.'

'The Teller he just wants to talk wid you is all.'

'Who?'

'My boss.'

'You must've made a mistake, sir – I don't know any Teller.'

He straightens, filling the hallway like a Russian tank. 'Of course you don't. But he knows you. An' he has information you want know. Yes?'

I stare into his face.

'If I let go your arm now you stop to be stupid?'

I lower my gaze.

He releases my arm.

I half turn, and then I spin back, punching him with all my strength in the belly. It's like hitting a hill. For a second I dance backwards in agony before the bodyguard wraps his fingers around my neck, attaching me to the chipboard by my windpipe. I fling out an arm, catching a trolley loaded with coffee cups and sending them crashing on to the carpet. The couple at the far end of the hallway turn. The bodyguard relaxes his grip, smiling for their benefit before dropping his voice to a hiss.

'Don't make me ask again. You come wid me, da?'

Moving his bulk to block the couple's view, the bodyguard grabs my left wrist, bending it backwards. I gasp in pain. I've got to do something or he's going to snap my arm in two. I kind of slump as if all the fight's gone out of me, and the movement drags him slightly off balance. Immediately I lift my right foot and stamp down on his ankle. His grip loosens for a fraction of a second and I take my chance. I lunge for the trolley, my hand slaps the coffee pot over – and scooping up the handle with my fingertips I twist my arm sideways and up, hurling the hot liquid into his face.

He falls to his knees, his hands flying upward.

I run. Believe me, I run. Flying down the hallway, I crash through a set of fire doors into a thick crowd of people. I start to shoulder my way through the crush and suddenly I find myself in a sweaty ballroom, a power ballad crashing over me like surf. Skidding across the floor, I ram right into a group of boys and one of them, a white guy with dreadlocks, launches himself at me, his fist bunching as he draws his arm back, but I move too fast, darting sideways and plunging into the crowd once more.

Battling my way to the edge of the dance floor, I twist around, just in time to see the bodyguard getting a meaty fist in the face from ol' dreadlocks. But he don't even seem to feel it – he shoves the guy to the floor like he's brushing off a kitten. He looks really pissed off. I watch, heart in mouth, as he reaches into his jacket and pulls out a pistol. And then, lifting his arm, he fires off a shot into the air.

Screams erupt from the dance floor and in a few seconds' time the music slews to a ragged stop. I turn, frantically searching for an escape route, but there's no door on my side of the room, just a long buffet table set close to the wall. I've got to pray it'll hide me for thirty seconds so I can decompress. I throw myself underneath, a rain of jalapeno peppers falling on my head as I squeeze under the tablecloth. Beside me a terrified girl whimpers from behind a jumbo bucket of chicken wings.

I peer out. My heart sinks. I've got no time. He's coming right this way. He's gonna see me for sure, all he's got to do is bend down. The room is now utterly silent, except for a faint mechanical bleep pulsing from the DJ's booth. Cigarette smoke curls up into the lights. I reach up to my visor with trembling hands. Maybe if I move *real* slow he won't see me.

'Psst.'

I freeze.

'Psst, Anthony.'

The sound comes from behind me. I turn my head. A few metres away is a large square air vent, set at the base of the wall. I peer forward into the darkness – only to see Lola's face staring back at me. I bite back a choke.

She chops the air. 'Come on! You *can't* decompress by yourself – you're on my Drop line, remember?'

My eyes widen. I hadn't thought of that. Now I'm really in the shit.

'Come on where?' I hiss.

'In here. Leads to the outside.'

Scarcely daring to breathe, I start to crawl towards her. The chicken-wing girl lets out a yelp. I put my finger to my lips . . . and she quietens down, staring at me with huge frightened eyes. And then I move again, till finally I'm pressed against the grille. The room is so silent all I can hear is the muted purring of the oxygen blowers and my breath coming in ragged gasps. He's gonna find me any second! I meet Lola's eyes.

She jerks her thumb. 'Open the cover.'

Grasping the metal grille, I start to ease it off its screws. It moves easy enough the first part, but then jams. I tighten my grip, trying to force it. It won't budge. In desperation I slam my fist against the vent and it slides free with a violent shriek that seems to fill the room. Flinging my head into the chute, I propel myself forward with the flats of my palms. My arms, my torso pass inside . . . and then . . . suddenly I'm stuck. I wriggle my hips, but I'm caught fast. Reaching around with my hand, I desperately search for what's holding me back. Shit, it's my belt buckle, my stupid belt buckle. It's stuck on the metal frame.

'C'mon!' Lola signals urgently from inside the chute.

I try to slide backwards to release the tension on the buckle, but I can't go that way either. I'm completely stuck.

'Anthony!'

There's nothing for it, I'm gonna have to try and rip myself free. I throw all my weight forward, my hands slam on to the cold metal and finally the buckle releases, whipping back against the chute with a great whang. It's the loudest sound I've ever heard. I breathe in, out, in . . . and then suddenly the wall shatters above my head. A bullet! He's seen me!

'Move!' Lola screams.

I lunge forward – and beneath me, suddenly, the shaft opens out – and I plunge down through the darkness, landing seconds later on a pile of trash outside the hotel.

I can just make out Lola beside me, her hands dancing over her deck as she commences our exit decompression sequence. As I watch, the thirty-second countdown pulses into life.

I clamber to my knees, gasp, 'How did you find me?'

'I tipped you down here in the first place. I knew you

were never gonna outrun him in the first hotel. Din't think he'd find you so fast.'

Her hand finds mine. 'Ready? It's gonna be bumpy.'

I grab her fingers.

The sound of smashing glass comes from above.

Lola rolls sideways. 'Get down!'

But it's too late. I stare up at the bodyguard. He leans out of a third-floor window, his gun trained directly on me. I lie, completely still, waiting for the shot, for the pain.

'You boy!'

I don't dare glance at him.

'Look at me.'

Slowly I turn my head.

He holsters his gun.

'Stupid boy. Only talk is all.'

And then the hotel walls blur, the neon sign coalescing into a lurid pixellated pink string

28, 29, 30 seconds . . . Out!

My eyes fly open. I'm back in Lola's bedroom; the air pressing down on me like an actual physical weight, crushing me like a rock on a bug. Nausea slops over me and I lurch over her bed and puke into the wastepaper basket under her desk. Then I spin round, scanning Lola's eyes for signs of life. She twitches, her eyes blank behind her visor. She's not out yet! And then her eyes fly open, her pupils dilating massively as she draws breath into her lungs in a great ragged pull.

I grab her by the shoulders. 'Are you OK?'

She pulls herself upright. 'What the . . . hell just . . . happened?'

'I don't know.'

'Well you seemed to have . . . pissed that guy off big . . . time.'

'I din't do nothing to him.'

'You must have.'

Suddenly her deck lights up with an incoming message. Lola scans the message and groans. 'What kind . . . of crazy is this?'

'What's it say?'

She flops her head back against the wall. 'You read it.'

I twist the deck towards me.

TELLER: Money must find a way to replicate. I only want to talk.

Lola shakes her head. 'Who the hell's Teller?'

'I don't know. The bodyguard guy said his name too.'

'You *must* know.'

'I tell you, I don't.'

Lola runs her hand through her red curls. 'I can't . . . do this now. I've got to bounce back to São Paulo . . . See if I've still got a job after I dived after you.'

'You can't, it's too dangerous.'

Lola fights to get her breath under control. 'It's money.'

'But what if that maniac comes after you too?'

She snorts. 'It's not me he's after . . . 'Sides, Anthony, as if he'd ever find me.'

'You sure?'

Lola's fingers move like a blur as she starts to spin herself a new Altform.

'Course. I'll be back out in a couple of hours . . . max.'

'Shall I stay here, watch over you?'

Her eyes meet mine. 'No. I'm cool. Bell you soon as I'm back and we'll talk. Promise.'

'Yeah?'

'Don't fret. He's probably just some freak jerking you around for kicks, or something.' She doesn't sound too convinced.

'OK.'

Lola settles herself against the wall and jacks back in. I watch as her eyes blur behind her visor, and after a few seconds I slump back on the pillows, as the adrenaline drains from my body. I'm totally wiped. Drop decompression on a good day finishes me off, never mind what we just went through. You've got to give yourself thirty seconds *minimum* to jump out or your brain just warps. At least, you do at the level Lola operates. She's been outsourcing herself abyss level for years now. The rest of the Debtbelt just do what we can in the Drop, hustling for work anywhere in the world we can find it. Legit or non legit. But Lola's strictly legit. No insider trading, no hacking and if a suit even thinks of laying a finger on her she jacks them out fast enough to give 'em the bends three days running.

As I lie there on her bed, suddenly I feel a vibration, a hum somewhere on my body. I pat my pockets and pull out my deck. It's my alarm. Damn! I'd forgotten. Thursday is my day to pick Stella up from Grandad's after college. I flop my head back down. I can't face moving again. But I've got to. I can't be late for Miss Stella Griffin.

Sliding my key into the lock of Grandad's apartment, I slip inside and pause for a moment to stare at my reflection in the hall mirror. My pale face stares back. I'm too serious. Man, I look *heavy*. I try curling my lips upward into a smile. Now I look mental. I've got to find a way to work the smile up into the rest of my face. Not an easy thing when you've just been hounded around a virtual São Paulo by a Russian maniac. I blow out my cheeks, I tell myself Lola's right . . . the bodyguard was just a random. It's over.

If I wasn't going to see Grandad I wouldn't even care about the quality of my smile, but he's got super X-ray vision – you just can't fool the man. I smooth my hair down, crinkle up my eyes like a shih tzu dog, but this makes me look like I'm on medication, the kind that makes you want to tell strangers your life story. No good. Shaking my head, I set off for the kitchen.

As I enter the room, I smile for real because from here I can see Stella in the garden, playing with our dog, Shane. I give her the old once over. She don't seem mad that I'm late. Good. Stepping over to the window, I bang softly on the glass and she looks up and gives a surprised wave. I jerk my thumb and mouth '*Let's go.*' I don't want to talk to Grandad today, not with what happened in the exam and with the Betta and Lola and all. I want to get moving. But then suddenly the study door opens and Grandad stands in front of me.

His face lights up. 'All right, Anthony!'

'Yes, sir.'

'I was hoping I'd catch you today. Come and tell me all about it.'

I frown. 'Ah . . . I can't, Grandad, I, er, promised Mom to get Stel back early today.'

His eyebrows lift. 'Well, you can give me just two minutes, eh?'

I plaster a smile on. I can't say no to him. I can't say no to a lousy two minutes, can I?

I follow him into his study and perch on a side table by the door for a speedy exit. Man, this place is mad. There are books and bits of drawing and paper all over the place and everything smells like wet Shane.

Depressing. I mean, I like dogs and all, but dirty wet dog smell makes me want to puke. Also Grandad's wearing this old fleece that looks like Shane's had some business with it. The man's a genius and he's dressing like some old bum. I don't like it when old people let it go like that. It's a bad sign.

I rub the back of my neck. 'I'm kind of beat. Can I tell you tomorrow?'

Grandad flicks a glance at me. 'Mr Griffin. Just sit yourself down and tell me how you think you did.'

I spread my hands. 'Fine. Good.'

He rolls his eyes. 'Is that it?'

I look down at the rug.

He sighs. 'I know you've got a lot on your plate, but it'll soon be done. Do you know where you'll be without this scholarship? Nowhere, son. Nowhere.'

'I know.'

'Completely nowhere. We couldn't afford to send you, not in a million years.'

I flick a bit of dirt off my sneakers. It drives me mad when people repeat themselves. Especially when you agreed with them the first time.

He's not giving up though. 'Well, did you at least get

the questions you revised for?'

'Yeah, mostly.'

'No big surprises, then?'

By this point I'm starting to get wound up. I flush. 'No, I told you.'

He glares at me, eyes turning icy. 'You didn't revise did you? You messed it up.'

I drop my gaze, whisper, 'Yes.'

'Goddamn idiot!'

Silence, just the sound of his raspy old breath as he fights to keep calm. I sit there, feeling really bad, like I've given him a heart attack or something. What a creep I am. I love my grandad. He won't go the way of other old men. My mom can't handle him; she just doesn't know what to do with him *at all*. She wants him to be charming like the twinkly old folk in daytime tube ads who want to take away the burden on loved ones by prepaying their own funeral costs. Fat chance. Grandad's more likely to set himself on fire like some kind of Viking berserker and hurl himself off a cliff.

I slide off the table. I stand up. I tell him he is one hundred per cent right and that I'm going to pull myself together. Starting *right now*.

He looks up, his eyes blazing. 'You can't let what happened—'

'Mess up my future, I know.' I try not to look at a long slop of soup on his fleece.

He rubs his white hair all backwards. 'You're too goddamn . . . young.'

And when he says that I feel kind of sick because he says it like I'm about to die or something. I kind of mumble goodbye and slip out the study, but when I shut the door behind me I lean against the doorframe for a moment and press my forehead against the wood. I used to love spending time here. Learning new stuff every day with Grandad; I used to suck it all in. It was the biggest high. Knowledge, information. I was such a kid. I squeeze my eyes shut.

I see the monitor, the multicoloured pulses as they flash across the screen, each jag representing different, secret functions. Blood pressure, heartbeat . . . intracranial pressure . . . I peer forward, I can't take my eyes off the subarachnoid bolt that's screwed through a hole in her skull. It rests on the surface of her brain, drawing off the fluid, releasing the pressure in her swollen head.

And when the paramedics arrive at the scene of an accident they use a thing called the Glasgow Coma Scale to tell how badly a person is hurt. And this scale goes from 3 to

15. And the lower the score the worse the news. And there are three determinants and they are:

Eye opening

Verbal responses

Movement

And the brain injury is termed mild when the person's score is 13 to 15. And a score of 9 to 12 is called moderate and a score of 8 or less is called a severe injury. But Tais, she didn't respond at all when they got to her.

And it's so weird because a human brain is the most complex known thing in the whole universe, but you look at it and it's just this 1.3 kilo soft grey pudding. I mean, *really*. You touch it and it feels like a chunk of sponge. But did you know that we've got basically three different brains, stacked up like Pringles inside our skull, and each one has a separate identity and intelligence? We've got stuff like different fear systems in different places. And half the time the different bits don't even talk to each other. They're like divorced people trapped in the same apartment *for ever*. That is some crazy madness to have going on in your skull for life.

And it's all because nature is lazy, right? I mean, let's say you're nature and X million years ago you knocked out a pretty decent reptile brain and you've got a bunch of snakes sliding around, breathing and eating, all chilled . . . But then one day you decide to take things up to a new level to, say, a lemur brain. A brain with a bit more style and *colour*, you get me? Well, if you're nature you ain't going to blow a few million years on a new monkey breathing system. That's long.

So what you do is create a new all-improved lemur midbrain and stick it on top of old snakey. And then a few millennia later when nature wants to step up a gear again to a great ape or a human, she goes and cooks up the neocortex of another brain and just slaps it on top of the others. It's amazing we can get out of bed in the morning if you ask me. I mean, that's a lot of madness squeezed into one tiny bony box, right?

But that's how it is for us. Me and you. Right now. Your snake brain's keeping your heart pumping, your lemur brain's giving you opposable thumbs to turn the pages, and your human brain's processing these words. We're a bunch of animals inside. And we think our brains are so superior, that we're apart from other creatures, but that's just not true. We're just the latest in a long continuum and who knows what will come next. And if you ask me, we ain't at all as smart as we think. And we could learn a lot from other creatures. I mean you'll never see an animal acting as though a dangerous situation is safe. Not like us at all.

As we leave Grandad's place, I turn to Stella. 'Let's go the back way today.'

Her hands freeze in the act of unwrapping a lollipop. 'Why?'

I shrug. 'Dunno. Feel like a change is all.'

'You did that last week too. What's wrong with the usual route?'

What's wrong is I don't want the Betta crew to come anywhere near my sister. It's taken her for ever just to build up the confidence to walk home with me at all.

I cut to the right, call over my shoulder, 'Come on, sis. Where's your sense of adventure?'

She stands surprised, but then she sets off at a skip to catch up with me, drawing level as I break down a side road.

'This boy, Juan, that's in my class slapped me when I was going to lessons this afternoon.'

I frown. 'Why'd he do that?'

'He hates me.'

'Why?'

'Because I laughed in the morning session when he couldn't spell spaghetti.'

'That's not cool. What are you . . . a kid?'

Stella rolls the lollipop around her mouth. 'No, but they always put me next to him in pair work. He smells funny.'

'Like what?'

'Cat food and ketchup.'

'Did he get into trouble?'

'No, I didn't tell anyone. I just put my 'phones on all afternoon. The others were all talking about the tube or their boyfriends or their favourite virts or whatever, so . . .' She suddenly puts her head on one side. 'I knew there was something wrong. Anthony, how come you're here? You're meant to be in an exam now.'

'Hey?'

'Three-thirty to five, Biology, Paper Two. It's on the timetable on your wall.'

I swallow, hard. I'm such a fool. I shouldn't have picked her up from Grandad's today.

'You've got the dates wrong, buddy.'

'No I haven't.'

I cuss myself for the stupid lie. Stella has a mind like a steel trap. She remembers *everything*.

She eyes me. 'You did *go*, didn't you?'

'I told you. You've got the—'

'You either didn't go or you left early!' Her hands fly to her mouth. 'You left *early*, Anthony!'

I cross my arms. 'I tell you, you've got it wrong – there was no exam today—'

'Liar!' Stella whacks me hard in the face with her lollipop; a sticky ball right on the bridge of my nose.

I grab her wrist. 'Ow! Quit it!'

'You're going to fail and not do the plan we worked out. Let go of me!'

'I'm not failing anything. Listen, Stel, I'm gonna let go of you, right, but no more hitting. And don't say nothing to Mom. OK?'

'Don't say nothing about what?'

'Nothing about nothing.'

'*Anything*. You can't say nothing about nothing. Your grammar sucks. *Let go*.'

'Not till you promise to keep quiet . . . and drop the lollipop too.'

She shakes her head. 'Only if you say you'll come to the crow park with me.'

I grab her wrist even tighter. 'Hey, we made a deal about that. You said you'd never go down there on your own.'

Stella squirms. 'That's why I'm asking you, dummy. And I don't want to go by myself . . . but you're always too busy. You say you'll come and then you don't. You've done that four times now.'

52

'But what are you doing down there?'

'Counting the new chicks.'

'It's too dangerous.'

She purses her lips. 'That's why I go at dawn. There's nobody about then.'

'I'm so gonna tell Mom.'

'Before or after I tell her about your exam?'

I told you, mind like a steel trap.

I sigh. 'Fine, I'll come with you. But you *promise* to keep quiet?'

She nods.

'And no more hitting me with that lollipop?'

She smiles.

I let go. Then she kicks me. Hard, right on the knee. I burst out laughing and for a moment I'm just me again, walking home with my kid sister on a Thursday like I always do.

Stella. She loves me and crows, not necessarily in that order. She kills me. And she's so pretty too. Right now she's in this phase of wearing a miniskirt with black tights underneath and a sparkly grey top that feels like barbed wire when I brush my hand against it. On the weekends she tops it off with a black and white Bedouin scarf, but never on a weekday. And another thing she's got going right now is a metallic purple heart on the back of her right hand that she keeps coloured in perfectly. And she's got what they call Cupid's-bow lips and a Milky Way of freckles swirling across her cheeks and nose. She's too much, she really is. I wouldn't change one thing about Stella.

Sometimes I hack into her account and I read this online crow journal she keeps. I know I ain't got no business there, but it's so weird and funny and cool I can't help myself. I'm really sly that way. That's why it's better you don't know me. I mean, what kind of creep hacks into his sister's private journal?

And y'know I wish there was something medical wrong with me. Then none of this'd be my fault. But you don't get any medication for feeling like the world don't make sense no more.

Take old Stella, she doesn't go round saying yes when she means no and talking crap about stuff she doesn't believe in. Not like normal people do. And who sets what's right and wrong anyway? Seems to me like the world is a place where a lot of people spend a lot of time pretending. And if you're like Stel, and you don't like pretending or you didn't ever learn how to pretend in the first place, then it's got to be given a name. Asperger's.

Crows are members of the Corvidae family and they live all over the world except for Antartica. They are scavengers and eat insects, frogs, mice, grains, burgers, KFC, pizza, even eggs and baby birds. Very loud and intelligent, crows are often viewed with loathing. Farmers think they are pests and many people fear them simply because of their black feathers, which they think are like death. This is ridiculous because research shows that crows are actually very caring creatures, and also among the smartest animals on the planet.

And I think they are better than people because I watch them a lot, at my grandad's and at a building site near the park where I am able to get close to them. Crows watch us much more than we watch them, for example White Tip recognises me when I come with peanuts in my pocket. Crows have a tight-knit families and they roost in big, big groups to protect themselves from enemies.

My favourite crows are White Tip and Hector. I think they are married but I can't tell because females and males look the same. Crows mate for life. White Tip is very bold and calls when s/he sees me coming. Then Hector flies over me low and when I put peanuts down they fly down and eat them. If other crows get too close to me they act aggressive but they are not aggressive with me at all.

Search

Categories
>Crow watch
>Crow artwork
>Crow tribe
>Crow worldwide

1	2	3	4	5	6
7	8	9	10	11	12	13
14	15	16	17	18	19	20
21	22	23	24	25	26	27
28	29	30			

A MURDER OF CROWS?

A group of crows is called a murder. People say this is because crows are seen as an omen of death but in fact the term 'murder of crows' comes from a time when lots of animal groups had poetic names.

And these names include: an ostentation of peacocks, a parliament of owls and a skulk of foxes.

This is funny and it shows people used to see and laugh with animals a lot more in olden times.

Painting done from photograph by S Griffin. White Tip and Hector on branch

55

But imagine a world where people didn't go round pretending all the time, then Stella would be normal, and in fact to go round saying one thing while thinking something opposite would be mad. Animals don't do it neither. Look at Shane. He's got emotions the same as me, but his are totally straight. When a dog is angry he's angry, when he's sad he's sad. You don't see no psychodrama in a dog. I wish I was a dog. I'd be one cool, hairy-arsed mutt.

I glance down at Shane, keeping pace alongside us. His flat brown eyes meet mine. Between you and me, he ain't the sharpest tool in the box. One time, after I'd been reading all this cool stuff about dog communication, I tried this thing of getting on his level, y'know with body language and play bowing because the reason us people get bitten by dogs mostly is because we've got bad dog manners. We do stuff like we stand right over them and look them straight in the eye. And then we reach out over their heads to pat them. These are all threats to a dog.

So like I say I was working away with Ye Olde Faithful Friend, trying to talk to him on a deeper level, but after a couple of weeks I kind of gave up. Total blank from Shane who, to be fair, had spent the previous five years as a furry waster and clearly wasn't up for turning into some seizure-sniffing dog genius just to please me. I can see his point of view. Or *maybe* that's just what he wants me to think and he is like, the Stephen Hawking of the dog world. Doubt it, though.

When we get back to the house, Stella runs upstairs and I go into the kitchen and make her favourite – Blackcurrant Jelly And One Scoop Of Vanilla Ice Cream (Not Touching). I dump the spoon in the sink and I'm heading up the stairs when they come swooping down on me . . . the *images*. Suddenly I'm *there*. Pinned, trapped in the moment.

All I can see is Tais. She is standing on the fifth floor walkway, outside apartment number 13, waiting to meet the man who left the voicemail message. She's knocked on the door a couple times, but no one's answering. She leans against the railing and gazes down over the Estate, wondering what to do. And then suddenly, from nowhere, a Betta pack slinks into the courtyard below. And they start to call up to her. Tais she starts to panic, she knows this ain't right. The Betta boys they aren't running, they're just walking, calling *Tais! Tais!* And this makes it worse somehow. It isn't the blind rage of the chase; this is a cold, premeditated hunt.

She starts to run. She climbs up to the next level, trying to find a way out, but by now they're everywhere. And she only has two choices. The first is she can jump off the walkway, but by this time she's on the sixth floor, pretty high up, and if she jumps, well she knows for sure she's going to get hurt, *bad*. It's a way to escape, but it's hard, you know, for her to make up her mind to jump like that, right over a railing into sure-fire pain.

And the second choice she has is to hide. But she doesn't have enough time. They are closing in. *Tais! Come here, come here!* So she starts to run again, desperate now. She makes it to the stairs, but she's out of time. They are on the walkway. They back her up to a far corner and surround her. They are all wearing masks. Tais is pleading with them, but they laugh in her face.

And then they start shoving her, saying *What you looking at, what you staring at?* And she is offering all her stuff to them, pleading with them, saying *Take my deck, take my credits*, y'know? But they don't care about that; they don't even look at what she's offering. And then she really gets scared because she knows there's not going to be any way out. She doesn't have anything they want, apart from her broken body.

But these are only images. I wasn't there. Some of it I've pieced together from what people told the feds, some of it is what I see in my mind. But I wasn't there. The only time Tais ever really needed me I wasn't there.

'Anthony, what are you doing?'

I blink. Stella is staring at me from the top of the stairs.

'Oh . . . nothing.' I start to climb again, fumbling with the ice cream bowl as I hand it to her. 'Here.'

I walk across the landing to my room and push inside, slumping against the jackets hanging from a hook on the door as I pull it shut behind me.

I let out a long, slow breath. I've had to learn to hold my nerve for when the past grips me. I've had to learn to breathe through it, to wait for the pain to pass. And it does pass. Eventually. And when it's gone I feel so good, so happy just to be alive. I don't know about you, if *you've* ever been through something really bad . . . but ain't breathing so sweet after? Like just being alive is the best gift you've ever had.

And maybe you're wondering how a geek like me came to hang out with people like Ali and Lola and Tais? Well,

I've told you how I came to know Ali, all that time ago. And later on when Ali hooked up with Lola, they both kind of let me tag along, but it didn't feel like tagging, no, I think they really liked me. I mean, we were a strange set of weirdos, each in our own way. Ali, the boy who couldn't be taught nothing and Lola who couldn't be taught enough. Him already working the street while she was hitting straight A's all the way. Maths and Physics and three languages and counting. Talk about opposites attracting.

And Tais? She was Lola's best friend. They used to work the Drop together, a lethal outsourcing partnership, pulling in money for their families, before Tais went her own way, that is. And when you first met Tais you might have thought she was in Lola's shadow because she was so quiet an' all. But later, once she let you in, she was just . . . so bright, so *dazzling*, y'know? In the way that almost no one ever is? But of course Tais din't pay me no mind, not when we first met. She barely looked at me, but I was hooked from day one. Totally gone. And from that day I set out to win her over. Boy that was some big job . . . but I never lost faith . . . No, I played the long game and I got there in the end.

And just out of interest, have you ever seen an adult male baboon? Those boys are built to fight, believe me, with massive chests and huge arms and long, curved canine teeth. But baboons are different from other primates because for the males, friendship is more important than fierceness as a way of getting the females. Basically, they make friends with females with reproductive payback in mind. Players, right? And so what I figured was what works for baboonanity could well work for humanity. I mean, we *are* family, right? I told Ali this once, and he let fly with a low whistle. 'Yeh. But it's one long, long way to get the girl, Anthony.'

So that's a bit of history for you. Oh, and the other thing is, I'm not a geek, I'm a coward. But I'm working on it, really I am.

Suddenly there's a knock at the front door. Crossing to the window I peer down. And then I pull back, *fast*. It's that detective guy, Daniel Garcia. I don't want to talk to him.

'Hello?'

Damn, I didn't duck fast enough.

'Anthony?'

A wild plan of escape fills my mind .... of running out the back and jumping the garden fence. But the detective knocks again, louder this time. I've got to face him.

Out on the landing, I push Stella's door open a crack.

'A policeman is here to see me. Stay up here, right?'

She lifts her eyes from her deck. 'What does he want?'

'Dunno. Just routine, I reckon. Just carry on with your journal, yeah?'

She sighs. 'OK, then.'

I trot downstairs, tucking my shirt in as I go. I open the front door and Detective Garcia smiles at me, a big guy in a shiny leather jacket.

'Can I come in?'

I flick a nervous glance along the street. I don't want anyone to see me talking to him.

He puts his foot on the top step. 'I'd like to go over some details in your statement again.'

I swallow. 'Can you do this without my mom here?'

He glances at his deck. 'You turned legal last week, didn't you?'

'Yes.' I sigh. Some birthday. I've blanked it already.

'Then you're good to go, son.'

He's trying to bully me, I know that, but the sooner I do this, the sooner he'll go away. So without a word, I turn and lead the way to the kitchen.

'All right to sit there?' Garcia moves towards the worn table in the centre of the room.

'Yes.'

He scrapes a chair back and sits. I watch as he punches

something into his deck with his great sausage fingers. Slowly I lean back against the kitchen counter, Ali's words echoing in my head. *'Them street feds, all they do is bust us nothing bottom of the ladder guys to make themselves look good, Anthony . . . They're a gang just like we are.'* And I never used to know what he meant, but now I'm getting an idea. I mean, look at this guy, picking on a schoolkid while the Betta who destroyed Tais walk free.

Garcia finally looks up from his pad, pasting a professional smile on his rubbery face with horrible results.

'So, Anthony. I'd like to go back over some details, specifically Tais' connection with the Betta. I know this is hard for you, but just do the best you can.'

'But I've told you everything I know already.'

'Well, I'd like to hear it again. In your own words.' He leans forward, lacing his fat fingers together. 'She was a gang member, right?'

I shake my head. 'No, you know she wasn't—'

'But she did work for the Betta?'

'Maybe . . . sometimes.'

'What kind of work?'

'We never talked about it.'

'You must know *something*.'

I run my fingers through my hair. I've got to at least

look like I'm cooperating.

'She – I think she did a little outsourcing for them.'

Garcia frowns. 'What do you mean?'

'Something to do with . . . data maybe.'

'What kind of data?'

I shrug. 'She hacked company data, stuff they don't publish. Internal plans, audits . . . that kind of thing.'

'And once she sourced this data she sold the information on to the Betta . . . for insider trading purposes?'

'Dunno about that side of things.'

He taps his deck. 'And how did she get so good at hacking through Drop company firewalls?'

'I told you, I've got no idea.'

'But you know she did it? You just told me about the hacking.'

'We spoke about it once. Max.'

'And you never saw her doing any of this? *C'mon*.'

An image of Tais comes into my head, her body curled tight, sweat dampening the sheets, her mind miles away in the Drop.

'Course not.'

'Do you expect me to believe that?'

I force my eyes to meet his, trying to control the anger rising inside me.

'I'm just a college student.'

'So was she.' Garcia suddenly shifts in his seat. 'And what went wrong? If she was doing such a good job why d'you reckon the Betta wanted to kill her?'

I shake my head. 'I told you. We *never* talked about the Betta.'

Garcia narrows his eyes. 'According to our report, you were the first on the scene after the incident . . . so you must've known something was wrong.'

'Yeah . . . she hit her deck alarm. I ran over there as fast as I could.'

'But it was all over by then?'

'Yeah. They were all running away.'

'And so you can't identify a single person at the scene of the crime?'

'No. They were all wearing bandanas or scarves. No faces.'

'Is that true, Anthony? I know you're scared, but . . . for Tais' sake—'

'Think I'd lie about this?'

His hand bunches into a fist. 'But how can you not have seen *anyone*?'

My anger bubbles up in my chest, stronger this time. I'm struggling to keep my voice calm.

'You know what a bandana is, right?'

'A bandana?' In his surprise his voice goes up high on

the *ana*, making the word sound Mexican or something.

'Yeah.' I watch him steadily.

'Of course I do.'

'So do you think you could recognise someone if they had a bandana over half their face? You think you could do better than me?'

Garcia rolls his eyes. 'Look, Anthony, this isn't all about you. This is hard on a lot of people and it's my job—'

I interrupt him. 'It's hard for you *why*?'

His eyes flash. 'Not all of us are bought off by the Betta, son. And the department's cut to the bone since the crash. I want to do this right, but I need *help*. D'you know how many of us are working homicide? Three for the whole city.'

'You didn't answer my question.'

'What?' His face flushes red.

I lean forward. 'Detective Garcia. All I'm asking is if you think you'd recognise someone if they had a bandana covering their face.'

His eyes bulge in disbelief, but he answers straight enough. 'No,' he says. 'Probably not.' After a long pause he flips his deck shut. 'I guess that's enough for today.' And then he pushes a hologram chip across the table.

'But if you think of anything, anything at all . . . you call me, right?'

After Garcia leaves, I stand in the hallway for a good fifteen minutes, the blood ringing in my ears. This rage inside me, it's starting to change me. I'd never have spoken to a fed like that before. Jamming the hologram chip into the flesh of my palm, I will myself to be calm, but it's no good, I'm falling again, I'm sliding downwards, and now I'm pinned, trapped in the moment when I ran into the Estate and caught sight of Tais' skewed body lying beneath the walkway. I ran over, I took her in my arms and I was calling her name, pleading with her to wake up . . . but she just didn't move. She just lay there like a doll.

And then, all of a sudden I wasn't alone. Someone was leaning over me. So close I could smell his breath. He bent down and whispered in my ear: *This ain't your thing, which is why I've been ordered to let you go. But you speak out and you're dead, boy . . . and your family too. Understand?* And then he made as if to punch me. I jerked to the left, landing hard on the ground – and when I righted myself again, he was gone. Twisting around, I caught a glimpse of a dark red Mustang accelerating across the parking lot, its tyres squealing dirty black on the asphalt as it left the Estate. It was just me and Tais left.

Her skull was smashed to pieces. The ambulance came and the whole neighbourhood flooded out. People were screaming, crying everywhere. It was the most attention she'd ever had in her life. That's funny. And so people were all weeping all over the place but nobody helped her while it was going on and by the time the feds rocked up it was way too late of course.

For days I wanted to come forward, but I didn't dare, I just didn't dare do it. I was shivering, I was shaking with fear. But in the end I had to step up. I mean, everyone had seen me there, with Tais in my arms, and Grandad was doing his nut, banging on about civic duty. So I sneaked down to the station and gave the feds a statement. But it was all for show, I didn't tell them what I really knew, about the voicemail, about the man who threatened me, about the Mustang. I figured what good would it do? And that's what I kept telling myself, but the truth is I didn't say anything because I was terrified they'd come after my family. I was sick to my guts with fear.

And I ain't even lying to Detective Garcia. I don't know what Tais did to make the Betta mad. But this is the Debtbelt and you don't cross them. Ever. Those are the rules. Even if the one paying is a college girl building up a few credits to keep herself in school and her family from going under.

And Tais was nothing to the Betta. But she was everything to me. Tais she hit me like she was a truck and I was road kill. Flat out. I spent a *year* just hanging out with her. I didn't want to kiss her, I just wanted to be with her. It sounds stupid, but it took me a mad long time to work out I even liked her so much.

Yeah, she was everything to me and now she's gone and all because no one can pay their debts any more and we all turned into junkers overnight. And it makes my old world seem so strange. Because once your credit's gone, there's no way back. You're toast. Leastways, you are round my way.

I bunch my fists. Nothing makes sense. Why is Tais worth so little and the Betta are worth so much? Who slapped a price tag on her like that? I mean, who started that? We walked out of Africa together, just a handful of us, and for millions of years nobody owned anything, nobody even understood what owning something *meant*. And now look at us. It ain't fair. Because if you'd known Tais, you'd have known she was worth much, much more'n any gangster. She was worth so much more than me, an' that's for sure.

And as I stand there, an idea it hits me. I'm going to work it out. What I'm worth. Running upstairs to my room, I snatch up my deck and start to punch in my search. I'm going to figure out a sum, do it fair and clear, y'get me? I'm going to work out my true value, in old-time dollars.

First I go for the elements . . .

Value of Anthony Griffin

1 x boy =

* 65% Oxygen
* 18% Carbon
* 10% Hydrogen
* 3% Nitrogen
* 1.5% Calcium
* 1% Phosphorous
* 0.35% Potassium
* 0.25% Sulphur
* 0.15% Sodium
* 0.15% Chlorine
* 0.05% Magnesium
* 0.0004% Iron
* 0.00004% Iodine

Total market value of Anthony Griffin elements = **Less than $1**

Which is just depressing. I mean, I've got to be worth more than that, right? So I change tactics and I go for the skin angle, because I reckon that's got to be worth a bit more. You know, with me being covered in fine kid leather and all. Now it turns out the average person has 5 to 6 square metres of skin (I am such a freak for researching this junior psycho killer shit). So I do a sum based on the current global market price of cowhide, which is $0.75 per square metre. And this adds up to the putrid sum of . . .

Entire skin of Anthony Griffin = **$4.12**

What a joke. I need to get serious here. I move on to my dead body. It turns out that the value of corpses is different in different places round the world, but a human skeleton for use by medical students, say, can fetch a few thousand dollars. And for a shrunken head I'd be looking at tens of thousands. Moving on up.

Anthony Griffin corpse/skeleton = **$3K–$10K**

But it's kind of a high price, you know, to actually have to *die* to get the cash. But there is a way around this . . . I could sell bits of my own body. Now it may surprise you to know that vital organs are no longer where the big money is. I mean, don't get me wrong, I'd still earn good money for that stuff too. Skin, tendons, heart valves, veins, lungs, kidneys and corneas . . . they're listed at roughly $100K. But if you want real money these days, bone marrow is where it's at. And if I sold all of my marrow I'd be looking at 23 million dollars, based on 1 kilogram @ $23,000 a gram. Decent, right? Or if I went down the DNA route I'd be looking at 10 million dollars, which ain't too shabby either. So basically if I sold myself off I'd be worth:

Bits of Anthony Griffin body = **$200K–$23 million**

But there's a catch. And it's a freaky one. I can buy body parts all day long, but it's totally illegal to sell myself. That's right. I can buy bits of other people but I can't sell bits of myself. Not directly. Well, not unless I check myself into some mafia-run hospital in the former USSR. So, I'm back to square one.

So then I start thinking about *work* . . . I'm not going to be a kid for much longer, so I change tactics again . . . I move on into the *future*. I mean, if I can drag myself out of the Dbelt and if I can be one of the lucky few to get a decent job then what am I worth over my lifetime?

74

Let's say I'm working 40 years. And let's say I average $50K a year.

Anthony Griffin working life = **$2 million**

That's good money, ain't it? But 40 years? That's a prison stretch. 40 years going into the office, chained to a desk. 40 years of hard labour. That's more'n you get for murdering someone.

I cross the room and, lying down on my bed, I wrap my fingers around the cool iridescent lid of my deck. I ain't exactly getting anywhere with this search. And then suddenly my sums fade away, as an incoming message flashes up onscreen.

TELLER: *Why did you run in São Paulo? I have information about Tais.*

My knuckles whiten around my deck. *Tais?* What the hell can this guy know about her? Or about what I know? Who is he? I rack my brains, trying to remember *exactly* what happened in the Drop. Closing my eyes, I see the sedan pulling up outside the hotel, the bodyguard jumping out, followed by that wealthy-looking guy. Is that the Teller? But if all he wanted to do was talk then why did he send his man to twist my arms off? I rewind the chase sequence in my mind, trying to see it from a different angle. Maybe the bodyguard only got mad because I wouldn't go with him . . . Maybe I blew my only lead.

I chew my lip. I *have* to talk to him. I've got no choice. I mean, after a month of searching for the voice I've gotten exactly nowhere. I'm desperate, man. I twist possible courses of action in my mind, but it always comes down to the same thing. The Teller will want to meet me in the Drop for sure – and to go in as *me* would be suicide. Even I'm not so mad as to go in without protection. No, the only way I can get that is to get a rock solid Altform – and the only person who can help me do that is Lola. My stomach twists. I'll have to tell her the truth. She'll never do it otherwise.

I jump up, pace the floor. I don't think I can do it. But there's no other way. For a full five minutes I stalk up and down my bedroom and then I snatch up my deck and punch in Lola's number, praying she's back from São Paulo. If she don't pick up now I'll never get up the nerve to tell her again. But she answers straight away. The girl is definitely worried about me, y'know, that I'm going to top myself or something. She normally never picks up on the second ring, believe me.

'Yeah?'

'Lola, the Teller messaged *me* this time.'

A swift intake of breath. 'He's good. To find you like that isn't easy, not on my Drop jack-in.'

'I think he's the rich-looking guy I saw outside the hotel in São Paulo.'

'But what does he want?'

'He says he doesn't want to hurt me, he only wants to talk about . . . Tais . . .'

Lola gasps. '*Tais?* What the—'

I cut in. '. . . And I think I maybe believe him. Remember when the bodyguard had the chance to shoot me and he didn't?'

'Woop de doo. Just cos the man didn't kill you, doesn't make him your new best friend. No way are you going back in. This Teller weirdo must've pieced you together with Tais from the press.'

I squeeze the deck in my hand. 'We could drop in Altform. Be safe that way.'

'*We?*'

'No one's better than you at cooking up a fake ID . . .'

Lola's voice lifts. 'No way! And look, if he knows something about Tais, why doesn't he take it to the feds? What's he coming to you for?'

'*Please?*'

A long pause. 'Why you want to meet him so bad?'

I ball my fist. I can't do it, not yet. I need more time to prepare.

'Meet me at the 333 Café? I've got to tell you something.'

'When?'

'Soon as you can. Tonight?'

'I can't get away. Earliest I can do is tomorrow morning.'

'Man, I can't wait that long.'

Lola's voice drops. 'What's going on?'

'I'll tell you if you come.'

'What if I don't want to hear?'

'Lola?'

She sighs. 'I hate you, Anthony.'

'So you'll come?'

'Yeah, but honest I can't come till ten tomorrow. We got a family thing tonight.'

'For real?'

'Yeah. I think my mom's finally gonna kill my brother's wife. She's ordered me to stay here as witness.'

'Ten tomorrow then, for sure?'

'Promise.'

Locking off, I let the deck slide from my fingers. And then somehow, like a gift from heaven, a rain of sweet sleep falls down on me and I smile, just as I begin to slip under. Tomorrow is another day – and I'm still in the game, right?

I'm hanging on by my fingernails from the edge of the walkway. I make a last desperate attempt to hold on to the rail, but it's no good, I can't get a grip on the smooth, cool metal. And now, inexorably, my body weight drags me down, pulling my hands, my fingers, away from the rail until, with a scream, I let go, plunging down towards the concrete courtyard below.

My eyes fly open. Light is streaming into my room through the open curtains. I struggle upright. I can't have slept all night can I? Snatching up my deck I check the time. 9.50! No! I'm late for Lola. Cursing, I jump out of bed and dragging my jacket on over my shoulders, I run out of the house. I don't even take the back roads; I just sprint straight up on to the main drag towards the 333 Café. I can't be late for Lola.

The café is where we all used to hang out. All four of us, back in the day. But since Tais, Lola and me have started to come here again, even if we can't afford it. The place is kind of a dump but it's got this old Hollywood feel to it, neon signs slung around the walls at rakish angles, flashing stuff like *Sunset Boulevard* and *Dream on!* – and along the back wall there's a framed poster for *Vertigo*, y'know, the Hitchcock movie poster, with a silhouette of a man falling into a silver spiral? I love that thing.

I give the owner, Ahmed, a quick hello before sliding into a padded booth at the rear of the café. He puts down his cup of heart attack coffee and waddles over.

'You all right, sunshine?'

I smile. 'Yeah, cool.'

His heavy black brows draw down. 'You look kinda rough.'

'Well I'm good.' I pump more air into my cheeks and stretch out my grin like I'm applying for a job at Disneyworld.

Ahmed cocks his head, unconvinced. 'You sure, kid?'

'Sure I'm sure. Look, can I get the Special, Ahmed?'

His eyebrows lift. 'What is it, your birthday or s'thing?'

I shake my head. 'No. Just feel like it.'

Ahmed slaps his order book shut. 'Okey dokey. Comin' up.'

I massage my jaw as Ahmed rolls towards the kitchen. You know to Russians, that Disney big smile is totally weird. Russians say '*Americans smile as if they are electric lights turned on.*' Russians talk a lot of sense if you ask me.

I sit, waiting, praying Lola will show. And after a few minutes the café door swings open and I look up. *It's her.* She's looking at me, her eyes scared. Scared for me. But as soon as our eyes meet she wipes the look off. Lola Rossi don't do *caring in a public place*. Striding over to my booth, she flings her bag down and scoots into the seat opposite.

'So, Antonio, we meet again.'

I narrow my eyes. 'Yes we do, Lolita.'

Ahmed shuffles back to our table. 'Voilà,' he cries, theatrically plonking two banana milkshakes and a bowl of hot fries down on the chipped tabletop.

Lola's eyes widen. 'The Special. You trying to sweeten me up or what?'

Swooping on a fry she drags it through a little dish of ketchup. For a second she holds it up between thumb and forefinger, then she shakes her head. 'Uggh, I hate my fat hands. Look at my fingers compared to this fry. Huge.'

I tut. 'You ain't fat. You know that.'

'Fries are a feminist issue, Anthony. Step away.' Lola

reaches forward and takes a hit on her milkshake.

'So what's up?'

I feel the blood rush to my face. I don't know how to start, so I'm just gonna have to jump in. 'What if I knew – something . . .'

Lola reaches for another fry. 'Details, please.'

I take a deep breath. 'Look, I didn't tell you this before, but I overheard a message left for Tais . . . just before the attack.'

Lola stops chewing. 'What did it say?'

'For her to come to apartment 13, fifth floor—'

She gasps. 'You've got this recorded?'

'No – I only heard it once . . . In Tais' room, the night before. When I remembered about it afterwards her voicemail was wiped.'

'By who?'

'I guess by whoever left the message. A man, kind of a southern accent by the sound of him.'

'Why din't you tell me before?'

I shrug, avoiding her eye.

'But you at least told the feds, right?'

'No. You're the first person.'

Her face goes slack. 'But why?'

'This masked Betta guy, he came over . . .'

'Where?'

'At the Estate. Just after the hit. I was bending over Tais, trying to stop the bleeding – and suddenly he was next to me. He told me he was gonna let me go free, but he'd come after me, after my family . . . if I caused any trouble.'

Lola drops her head in her hands. 'Oh, Jesus.'

I stare at her in silence.

She straightens. 'But how is this Teller weirdo connecting this to you?'

'Dunno. Unless somehow he knows what I've been doing.'

'And what's that?'

'Patrolling the Betta hideouts, y'know – the Estate, the woods, the mall. Searching for the guy who left the message.'

'Is *that* where you've been?'

'Yeah. But there's no way the Teller could know that, right?'

She pushes herself back from the table. 'You idiot. You could've gotten yourself killed.'

'Yeah well, I didn't. And I've not found a thing. That's why I've got to take this chance . . . this guy *knows* something for sure.'

'But what if it's a trap? The Betta testing you out, to see if you'll stay quiet?'

I swallow. 'That's why I'm asking you to help me.'

Lola shakes her head. 'This is some heavy shit. Can't you find a way to tell the feds in secret—'

'No way. The Betta will find out. You know how it is.' I press my hands flat on the table. 'Lola, I just want to find out the *truth* . . .'

Lola toys with her straw. 'You never even go and see her any more.'

I swallow. 'I can't . . . you know I can't.'

'No, I don't know.'

I sneak a glance at Lola. I'm scared to tell her. I'm scared she'll laugh.

Lola lifts her eyes and she's not laughing, she's watching me, quiet, intense.

I swallow. 'I . . . let her down so bad . . .'

'What are you talking about?'

'I should have told the feds the truth, and it's too late now.'

She snorts. 'And pointed the finger at a Betta leader? You're right, your family would be dead.'

'I know, but . . . I can't go on like this.'

Lola's face blurs. 'I'm so angry with her. Look at what she's done to you . . . to all of us. What did she think she was doing, hacking for that bunch of thugs?'

'You know why she did it.'

She holds my gaze for a fraction of a second. 'Don't do that. We're all in the shit as bad as each other. Look at your family . . . mine too – but what we do's legit. No, Tais she made a choice to go that way.'

I watch her, wondering if she knows the truth. Maybe she does, maybe she doesn't *want* to know.

Lola swirls her straw slowly inside the Coke glass.

'And what if I say no?'

I look down at my hands, my fingers white on the tabletop.

She sighs. 'You'll go inside alone, right?'

'Yes.'

Lola runs her hand across her face. 'Then that's it. I ain't losing you as well. Show me the message.'

Digging into my pocket, I draw out my deck and twist the screen to face her. Scanning the Teller's message slowly, she purses her lips.

'Well then, down to business. Let's start with the most important question, right?'

She hits *re>message*.

LOLA108: How do we know we can trust you?

In the 333, the seconds tick by. We sit in silence, the only sound a commercial on the tube. Despite myself my eyes wander over to the screen. Maybe it's the stress, but my brain suddenly feels like a vacant lot.

Onscreen there's some kind of fitness workout going on. The 3D fitness trainer is stressing *overall tone* over *bunchy* muscles. '*Bunchy is bad*,' she says, flexing a tiny bicep right into my face. I like the tube. It relaxes me. Especially the makeover shows, y'know, where they make everything better than it was before in half an hour? But I get really wound up in the advirts, especially the ones where they animate the animals who've been killed to make the thing; like when tuna start rapping about filet-o-fish. That ain't right.

Suddenly the deck vibrates and I jerk, sending my milkshake spinning across the table. Lola leans forward, reads.

TELLER: *You don't know if you can trust me, but you can. I will send you neutral coordinates for a Drop meet.*

Lola hits *re>message* again.

LOLA108: *No bodyguard. No violence.*

TELLER: *Agreed. Just talk.*

LOLA108: *When?*

TELLER: *Now?*

Lola looks up, eyes wide. 'What do you reckon?'

My heart starts to thud fast in my chest. 'Yes. We've got to take the chance.'

'You trust him?'

'Don't know. But at least we've got your Altform as protection.'

Lola shakes her head. 'Altform is just a cover, it's not armour.'

I smile. 'It is the way you do it.'

Her eyes narrow as she looks over at Ahmed.

'What about him?'

I twist my head. The café owner sits hunched, half asleep over his paper in the corner.

'He won't pay us no mind.'

Lola sighs. 'I'm going to say yes and then check out where the Teller's coordinates point to before I decide to jump.'

'OK.'

She leans forward, types.

LOLA108: OK. Ready.

After a few seconds the return message flies in.

TELLER: These are the coordinates. You have two minutes before they burn.

A long stream of digits slides across the screen. Lola immediately activates a spectrum search, tapping her fingers as the deck strobes through a three-sixty zone raid. Her hand suddenly tenses on the keyboard.

'He's in Moskva Citi.'

'What's that mean?'

'Tons of super powerful hedge funds are based there, y'know, the kind of people who bring whole currencies down.'

I swallow. 'Is that good or bad for us?'

Lola frowns. 'It's a weird place to pick for a neutral meet.'

I glance at the time. 'C'mon. We've got to make a decision. Let me Drop alone if you don't want to come.'

She holds up her hand, grinning. 'Na-ah. Chill, Anthony – I din't say I wasn't coming. Just wanted to know where we were going. Let me spin, now.'

I grip my visor in my hand, watching Lola spin the Altform IDs, her fingers speeding over the deck as she twists the Drop code, rerouting our data through a thousand entry and exit points. It takes a special kind of mind to do this, believe me.

And then she looks up.

'You ready?'

I lift my visor to my face.

Lola holds up her forefinger. 'One rule, tho'. If I say we jump out, we jump, right? No backchat.'

'Right.'

I give the café one last check. Ahmed is dozing for real now. Taking the deck 'trodes, I attach them to my temple. And then Lola Rossi punches us in.

Fssst! Sparks spin out into the blackness. A sharp flash jags through the dark, temporarily lighting up the interior of a curved train carriage. Grabbing a rail, I yank myself upright from the floor. Opposite me, Lola sprawls across a row of seats, her head bent as she comes out of the jump. At least I think it's Lola.

For a long moment I stare at her alien face as the train barrels up out of a tunnel on to the surface. Dark, flowing hair and a total face resculpt; her face is brand new – wide Asiatic cheekbones and sensuous mouth, along with a new name, birth date, location, DNA records. Lola Rossi is the queen of Altform, all right.

Turning to the window, I try to catch a glimpse of my own reflection, but all I can make out is a brief flash of my strange, dilated black pupils and golden skin as the train rattles through the flickering lights of a platform. Once again we emerge on the surface and I peer out of the window. We've now entered a kind of gleaming chrome and glass valley with skyscrapers towering overhead. This must be Moskva Citi.

I reach out, touch Lola's wrist. 'You all right?'

She lifts her eyes. 'Uh-huh. I was just checking our position. We're good, nearly dead on the coordinates.'

The train dives underground again, boring through the tunnel at electrifying speed, but as it enters a curve, a grinding metallic scream fills the air and our carriage jerks violently. Thrown back against my seat, I cover my ears with my hands as the brakes bite on the tracks, the friction of metal against metal filling the air with an intolerable sound until, with a final ear-splitting wail, the train grinds to a halt.

After a moment I rise to my feet. 'You think this is it?'

'Go and look. Be careful,' Lola growls from the far end of the carriage where she's been flung. I cross to the doors, hit the release button and look out on the deserted platform. It's hard to see much; the only light comes from dull orange back-up bulbs set high on the tunnel walls. Suddenly a platform speaker hums into life and a ghostly polyphonic tone bounces off the tunnel walls, followed by a female voice announcing something in sharp, clipped Russian. And then silence falls again.

Lola comes up behind me. 'I don't like it.'

'Maybe we're meant to get off here?'

'If this guy is on the level why are we meeting in some shitty underground tunnel?' She taps her deck. 'I'm gonna take us out if I don't see something soon.'

I hold out my hand. 'Wait. We din't come all this way just to bail without looking around.'

'Two minutes. If I don't like it, we're out.'

I jerk my thumb sideways. 'Let's try left. There's some kind of a light down there.'

Lola nods and we make our way along the dim platform. After groping forward for a while, I pull up, peering into the gloom ahead.

'It's coming from inside a room . . . The door's open . . . there, see?'

Speeding up, we arrive near the open door, pausing a metre short of a flickering pool of light that spills on to the platform. I inch forward and look inside. Lit only by a bare light bulb swinging from the ceiling, the walls are blank concrete, the floor grey tiles marked with some kind of company insignia. I take a tentative step through the doorway. The room is an L shape, and I can just make out a worktable with four tatty stools around the corner.

I clear my throat. 'Hello?'

I look back at Lola. She shrugs.

'Hello?' I take another step, Lola close behind me.

Suddenly someone shoves us from behind, sending us sprawling to the ground. Struggling to right myself I whirl around. The bodyguard stands behind us, pistol in hand.

Lola shouts, 'I'm taking us out!'

'Wait!' A man emerges from the shadows at the rear of the room.

Lola turns her gaze on him. 'Are you the Teller?'

'Yes.'

'You said it was just you.' Her finger taps on the decompression button.

The Teller holds his hands out. 'Please. I mean you no harm . . . I had to take precautions too – you might have been a trap.'

I look him up and down. It's the guy from São Paulo all right.

'It's him, Lola.'

The man's gaze flicks to me.

'Anthony?'

Blood rushes to my face. 'Yes.'

'Stay, please. On my word I mean you no harm.' He looks over my shoulder. 'Vassily! Gun down.'

Lola's finger moves slowly from the button. I lean

against the table, my eyes never leaving the man's face. I see now that he's not bald but shaved, a perfect number one cut. I wonder what he looks like in reality. Here he's perfect. Loaded for sure; his forehead is high and smooth, his nose a perfect aquiline job. His eyes, clear amber, meet mine. A piercing glance – it feels like I'm being weighed, down to the last milligram.

I nod, slowly.

'Thank you.' The Teller gestures to the bodyguard, who immediately bends and picks up a slab of heavy polycarbonate that gleams like dull silver. He turns and wedges it against the substation door.

Lola frowns. 'What's that?'

'It's a jammer. It'll keep us secret, for a short while at least.'

I bend towards him. 'Who are you?'

The Teller shakes his head. 'I cannot say. All you need to know is I'm a friend.'

'So why were you trying to kill me in São Paulo?'

'Why did you run? I only wanted to talk with you.'

'Have you seen the size of your bodyguard?'

A brief smile tugs at the corner of his lips. 'Yes, well, Vassily can be quite . . . *intimidating*. I apologise.'

Lola keeps the table between her and the Teller. 'Who do you work for?'

The Teller shrugs. 'Generally, for whoever hires me. But right now I'm here on my own behalf. To pass on information . . . about Tais. She was your friend, no?'

I swallow. '*Is*.'

He shoots me a look. 'Once again, I apologise. I deal in information. I buy, I sell, I search, I trace. I didn't know your Tais in the real world, but in the Drop often we would pass on things of . . . interest to each other.'

'Like what?'

He shrugs. 'That is not permitted to speak of—'

Lola cuts in. 'So why do you want to speak to us?'

The Teller steeples his fingers. 'I want to tell you something about Tais' last job. She was paid to run a highly sophisticated hack on a company called Inspire – on behalf of a consortium called Star Holdings.'

'Are they owned by the Betta?'

'I don't know. Even in the real world market it's hard to know who owns what . . . not to speak of the layers of misinformation and lies you find inside the Drop.'

I frown. 'But for sure the Betta must've been involved . . . Otherwise why would Tais be in there?'

He nods. 'Yes, in some way. Anyway, let me return to my story. Tais, after months of painstaking work, had punctured through Inspire's security core, yes? She was now ready to pass on their confidential files to Star

Holdings – but at this point she discovered something she did not expect to find.'

'She told you this herself?'

'Yes.'

'Why?'

'Because, I told you . . . we passed on information to each other. Please, we will not get far if you keep interrupting like this.'

I frown. 'So what did she find?'

'Well, first I have to tell you why Star Holdings wanted the information. Star are a breaker corporation. They specialise in smashing up companies and selling the parts off to the highest bidder. They were about to mount a takeover bid for Inspire and they wanted to get the inside track on what parts were unprofitable, what companies they would ditch immediately. You follow?'

I nod. 'Yeah, but Tais, you were about to tell us what she found . . .'

'That one of the unprofitable companies under Inspire was a major employer in your city. That Star Holdings were going to shut them down for sure, with mass redundancies in a matter of months – thousands of jobs gone in a city that can't afford to lose even one. And that's when she contacted me for help. She wanted to sabotage Star Holdings' takeover bid, prevent the bid.'

'And what did you say?'

The man's amber eyes darken. 'I blanked her of course. Way too dangerous for me . . . And then a week passed, and then another and I noticed that she wasn't active any more. And so I ran a trace, a deep one, only to find out her data was filed as static.'

'What does that mean?'

'Non-*operational*.'

'And you think it's because she contacted you?'

He shifts restlessly in his seat. 'I don't know for sure. Could be it was something else, unrelated . . . but my gut feeling is someone was watching . . . someone who decoded her communication with me.'

The bodyguard suddenly signals from the door. 'There is sweep search coming.'

Lola frowns. 'Who's that?'

The Teller waves his hand. 'Could be anyone. Maybe we are being watched now . . . or . . . maybe it is a routine sweep. Happens all the time in Moskva Citi. There is no one more paranoid than a dirty financier.' He smiles, before glancing at his deck. 'We must be quick. So do you wish for my help?'

I lean forward. 'Why are you offering *now*?'

He looks down, examining his immaculate fingernails. 'You know when Chimerica blew, that week the New

York stock exchange lost three hundred points a day for seven days in a row . . . ? That's a twenty-sigma point move. Do you understand how unlikely that is?'

I shake my head. 'Nope.'

'It's almost impossible to put into words, but if you imagine that the New York stock exchange had been trading every day since the Big Bang, the odds would still have been against it falling like that.' The Teller's eyes blaze. 'That's how screwed up the models the financiers were using were. And now it's like they don't even care, they just carry on, business as usual.'

'But what's that got to do with Tais?'

'A Debtbelt girl has no business being caught up in their mess.'

The bodyguard twists around. 'One minute, sir, and we must jump. Worms now hacking into the jammer.'

Lola shakes her head. 'Tais chose the life.'

The Teller looks at her, curious. 'Do you mind if I ask how old you are?'

Lola meets his gaze steadily. 'Old enough.'

'I doubt that.'

She shrugs. 'No choice, boss. A Debtbelt girl has got to eat.'

The Teller stands, abruptly. 'Time is out. And so I will tell you simple. I – I – want to help . . . because . . . if I don't I'm as dirty as they are. I won't break cover, but I will help you find who owns Star Holdings, give you something to take to the authorities.'

'How will you do that?'

'The takeover happened last week. Star bought Inspire and no doubt right now they're executing their break-up plans. That we can do nothing about, but it *does* mean we can find out who's behind them.'

'How?'

'For a takeover deal to be legal there must be a credit transfer deed, a document with a name on it, a *real* person at the head of a company who has underwritten the risk. Even in the Drop there must be this thing.'

'And where would we find a deed like that?'

'In Geneva, in a sealed digital vault deep inside the Drop corporation administrative complex. Every single company registration deed is stored there by law.'

The bodyguard raises his voice, urgent. 'Sweep closing in. Time for out. Now!'

The Teller glances at Lola. 'Begin your decompression.' And then he pushes a piece of carefully folded paper towards me.

'These are the coordinates for Geneva and the access codes for the vault box where the documents are stored. You still must break in, but these will help.'

I reach forward for the paper. 'But how are we going to do that?'

He nods at Lola. 'Ask your friend. She's good.'

I scoop the coordinates up. 'Thanks.'

'This information cost me dear. Keep it safe.' The Teller holds my eye for a moment. 'Good luck.'

I gaze into his face for a moment – and then suddenly the concrete walls begin to buckle, the table slanting away from me at a sickening angle.

28, 29, 30 . . .

My hands are pressed hard against the studded faux-leather booth in the 333 Café. Opening my eyes I see the fitness trainer again, still pumping her tiny biceps into camera.

I turn to Lola, scanning her anxiously, waiting for life to flood back into her face.

She shakes her head. 'Wow.'

'What do you reckon?'

'I don't know. I'm going to have to run a whole bunch of checks on the Geneva coordinates.'

'But what about what he said Tais was doing? That it wasn't just a hack . . .'

Lola holds up her hand. 'Let's wait and see.'

Deep inside my pocket, I feel a vibration. I pull out my

deck, read the message.

'Ah, no.'

'What is it?'

'It's Mom. She wants me to pick Stella up from school. She can't get away from work.'

Lola frowns. 'What happened?'

'Dunno exactly. One of the other kids puked up and Stella's freaked out. I've got to go.'

I stand up, groggy.

Lola's voice is suddenly gentle. 'Want me to come with?'

'No, I'll handle it.' I slide the coordinate paper over to her. 'But call me soon as you find anything out?'

'I will.'

'And Lola?'

'Yeah?'

'Thanks.'

She gives me a long, slow look. 'It isn't only you who cared about her, you know.'

Outside the café, I stand for a moment on the traffic-choked street corner and draw in a lungful of carbon monoxide. I've got to make myself calm and cool for Stella, clear my mind of Tais and the Drop and focus only on her. That's how it's got to be.

I set off for the train station. The train's just pulling in as I arrive, so I run down the stairs and jump into the last carriage as it sets off again. The place is packed out, hot as all hell. I try to move away from people, to get me some air, but there's no space and so I find myself pressed up against a woman, staring into the face of a miniature dog she's holding in her arms. It's one of those dogs that looks like it's been peeled. I turn my head, trying to avoid its tiny hotdog breath on my face.

But a dog is a tame wolf and we've been together for thousands of years, first with wolves and then with dogs, back when we were nothing more than a band of roaming chimps and the deal was much more equal. And back then we weren't so cocky, I can tell you. We were just moving from Homo erectus to Homo sapiens; a bunch of small brainers who sort of got lucky and joined up with the wolves to hunt. And here's the really good part – it was the wolves that were the brains of the outfit initially. They really lit a fire under us. Suddenly I think back to what the Teller said about the financiers and their stupid sums. What makes us think we're so intelligent? What an arrogant bunch we are. The Aborigines they say *Dogs made us* but no one else remembers. If I was a wolf I'd be super mad about this.

I press myself against the window, rub my eyes. I'm still weirded out after the Drop. Feels like I've got one foot in there and one in the real world. The train curves past a row of trees and through the leaves I can just make out the Estate, huge and grey. Me and Ali used to hang out there all the time. I remember one day we climbed all the way up to the roof. It was a beautiful spring morning with the city laid out smooth beneath us and I stood next to Ali as he spun around, slow, on his scuffed sneaker heel, arm rotating like a compass arrow as he gave me a tour of the neighbourhood.

At each new position of his arm, he'd tell me the names of the gang whose territory it was, and their size and alliances. The Betta, the Level 2 cru, the Virus – Ali had a head for detail, all right. He made me feel like a stranger in my own city because back then I din't know about no gangs, not really. All I knew was we were two tribes of humans, one living one life, one living another. One legit and one underworld. But that was before. Now we're all living the same life. And the Betta have muscled up through the other gangs, from street level all the way up to the top. Credit, not drugs – that's where the action is now. Short-selling, junking, gold farming, black boxing, risk-rolling – the Betta got a finger in every pie. That's how Tais got sucked in. And I can't believe we've let whole cities slide like this, with everybody living in this fear state. The lost generation, that's what they call us. Joke, right?

I still live in the same area as I ever did, right, but my angle, my arc is flipped one degree. I can't focus any more. It's like when you go for an eye test, yeah, and the optician drops a lens into that heavy slot thing covering your eye. And as he changes lenses he goes *Is that better or worse? And now? And what if I do this? Sharper? Fuzzier? And now? Better or worse?* That's what it feels like.

I
AM SCR
EWED I D
ONT BELO
NG AN
YWHER
E NO
MORE

The train pulls into the next stop and I clatter down the steps and take a left turn towards Stella's school. A minute later and I'm outside the gates, gazing through the railings at the building, a great shaggy pile of a place it is. Stel shouldn't be here, she's a million times smarter than anyone in a ten-mile radius, but her special place shut last year. I had a mate, Bomber, who went there, too – God knows where he is now. He had a dodgy chromosome thing that gave him a weird-shaped head, with like a ridge down the middle. Everyone called him Strawberry Head. He was thrown out of my school for being a crazy one. He was always starting riots in class, but when he wasn't being mental he was genius. Funny as all hell.

But then his mom put him on Ritalin or something, and totally flattened him right out, like a pancake. A zombie pancake. Fat and flat. I never knew anyone eat so much junk as Bomber did, once the drugs kicked in. He was on the munch all day long, ten packs of M&Ms easy. But he'd never touch the blue ones, said they made him crazy. Used to give 'em to me whenever he saw me. Said he needed to keep away from the E numbers. That was before he stole a street sweeper and rammed the doors of a shopping mall, mind. Bomber was a riot.

I like it when all the madness is out in the open, where you can see it. Not like us. Stella though, she shouldn't be in this run-down hole. No one should. It's like when on nature documentaries they go: *You might think no life can exist in this inhospitable hydrothermal vent, but you'd be wrong. At 120 degrees centigrade this is the hottest place on earth and yet it's home for someone, a remarkably tough little species – the tiny prokaryote.*

Stel, she should be doing her exams now, not waiting two more years. But that kind of education costs money, y'know? That's why I want to be a professional, a scientist, something with animals, so I can look after her properly later. That's the plan, me and her have got it all worked out. At least we did till I started messing up.

Signing in at the security desk I take the stairs two at a time up to the second floor, to her base area. It's deserted. I peer out of the window, there are some kids I recognise from her year group down on the playing field, doing half-assed star jumps. Stella isn't with them, so my guess is she's in the cloakroom at the end of the corridor. That's her usual hiding place.

I set off along the corridor. Reaching the final door, I shade my eyes to block my reflection and stare through the pane of circular glass. There she is, hunched up in the far corner. She's wearing a too-big tracksuit from the spare clothes locker; the extra fabric is bunched up round her neck. She's bent over her deck. She's typing, real fast, like she's not writing real words. She's super pale. I've got to keep calm or I don't know what I'll do. I'd take all the pain for her if I could, I really would, you know.

I push the door open.

THE MIRROR TEST

Magpies are crows and they're very smart. Elephants and dolphins and primates and human babies by the time they're two can see themselves, but no one ever knew that a crow could. They do loads of things better than higher mammals and they don't even have a neocortex. It's a mystery, It's like the opposite of what everybody thought they knew about brains and it shows we dont' understand very much at all.

Stella Griffin blog

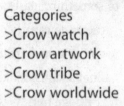

Categories
>Crow watch
>Crow artwork
>Crow tribe
>Crow worldwide

M	T	W	T	F	S	S
	1	2	3	4	5	6
7	8	9	10	11	12	13
14	15	16	17	18	19	20
21	22	23	24	25	26	27
28	29	30				

'Hey sis, it's me.'

Stella doesn't look up.

'Stel?'

She doesn't turn.

I move over to her side. 'Let's get you home and into your own clothes, yeah?'

Her eyes are glued to her deck screen. I've got to think of something, fast.

Leaning over her shoulder, I tap the screen.

'Who's this bird then?'

Stella sighs, looks at her sneakers.

I nudge her. 'Well?'

She shrugs, but she's about to crack, I can feel it.

She leans towards me, imperceptibly.

'I – I don't know his name.'

'Well, why's he got a yellow sticker on his chest?'

She tosses her head.

'Hmm? Is it an experiment?'

I gaze down at the top of her head. I'm the slyest fox on the block and I know how to get my sister talking. *Crows.* I start to count silently inside my head. She can't hold out for much longer . . .

'He's doing the Mirror Test,' Stella suddenly blurts out.

I keep my voice level. 'What's that then?'

'It's when they put a sticker on the magpie's chest and

then stand him in front of a mirror.'

'What for?'

'Because if he notices the mark and tries to peck it off that means he can see himself. That he's *self-aware*.'

'And does he see the mark?'

'Yes.' Stella nods, thoughtful. 'Of course. Magpies are crows and they're very bright. Elephants and dolphins and primates and human babies by the time they're two can see themselves, but no one ever knew that a crow could. They do loads of things better than higher mammals and they don't even have a neocortex. It's a mystery, Anthony. It's like the opposite of what everybody thought they knew about brains.'

I try to take her hand, but she pushes me away. 'You're all stupid.'

'What happened, Stel?'

Her voice is scarcely above a whisper. 'They make fun of me because I don't know how to look them in the eye. And then Leo made himself puke to freak me out.'

Her eyes are puffy from crying. She turns to stare out of the window again. Blank. She used to be so bullied, to the point where she wanted to hurt herself. Kids wound her up and she didn't know how to calm down. She was one big meltdown. She couldn't control it and it hurt her so much. She's getting better now, but man, it just kills me when she's in pain.

And you know what's funny? When people say autistic children are in their own little world. And there's this autistic savant guy in London, Stephen Wiltshire, yeah, and one time they flew him over the City in a chopper and when he landed he picked up a pen and created a ten-metre long drawing of the skyline from memory. And it was perfect. Perspective, scale, detail. Everything. And how he does it is simple. He draws exactly what he sees.

You'd think that'd be the most easy thing in the world, right? To see. But it ain't. Us normal human beings *can't* see what's in front of us. We've got too much neocortex in the way and we sort of melt stuff into concepts and in the end all we ever see is our *idea* of reality. And our brains *can't not* melt stuff. It's like we've got a permanent filter switched on upstairs. And this is what we call normality. But the trouble with it is we only see what we *expect* to see. And it seems to me we need to learn to bypass our own brains, to learn to open our eyes again. And we could do it too, I reckon. Human brains are amazing.

Suddenly an image of Tais rises up before me so vivid, her pale face lying on the pillow. What's she feeling, what's she thinking, *right now*? I jam my fingernails into the palm of my hand. Got to keep calm for Stella.

'Anthony!'

I blink.

Stella points towards my jacket pocket. 'Your deck is buzzing.'

I yank the device out, flick it on. It's Lola, her flushed face coming into focus on the screen.

I turn away, whisper, 'Yeah?'

Her voice is breathy with excitement. 'Teller's coordinates check out. He's given us the Drop administrative headquarters in Geneva. Top secret location – we'd have never found it ourselves.'

I bite back a choke. 'For real?'

'Yeah. And not only that, he's given us *two* sets of numbers. One to access the building and one to open the vault. This guy is seriously good.'

I frown. 'What? So we can just cruise in there and get the name on Star Holdings' records? Seems too easy.'

'No, we've still got work to do. The coordinates point us to the location, that's all. We still have to break in. There's no way a couple of kids like us'd be allowed to roll in, no matter what Altform I spun around us.'

'So what are we gonna do?'

Lola grins. 'I'm going to bring in some of my circle to create a diversion.'

'Who?'

'Just call them my Associates . . . kids from across the

Debtbelt I work the Drop with . . .'

'But they ain't Dropping into Geneva with us are they? This is our deal, right?'

'Yeah, chill. But we'll need backup for sure.' Lola pauses. 'Anthony?'

'Uh-huh?'

'You sure you want to come? I mean you're not exactly built for inside work.'

'I'm coming.'

'But—'

I ball my fists. 'I'm *coming*, Lola.'

She sighs. 'OK. But same rules as before. If I don't like something we bail. Yes?'

'Yeah.'

'Come to mine later, after college?'

'Deal. 'Bout five?'

I hang up and when I turn around, Stella is looking at me, her eyes sharp as a magpie in a mirror test.

'Where are you going at five?'

I stuff the deck back into my pocket. 'Hey Big Ears, I'm not going nowhere.'

She sighs. 'You can't *not go nowhere*. Your grammar is terrible.'

I grin. 'Yes it is. Now come on, let's go home.'

Up in her bedroom, Lola positions herself on the bed, her back pressed up against the wall.

'Ready?'

Tightening my visor, I glance up at the wall clock. 5.25.

'Yes.'

Lola's fingers move over her deck – a roll of sound and colour curves over me – I take a deep breath and dive – and suddenly I'm standing in a winter park, encircled by heavy, grand buildings. I turn, looking for Lola, and catch a glimpse of her red mane of curls, but before I can make my way over to her, my visual input blurs again and I'm jerked deep in to the heart of a high-tech business district.

For a moment I stand, dizzy, at the base of a soaring five-hundred-floor building. Steadying myself against the wall, I wait for the next move, but after a few seconds it's clear we've arrived. Drop Geneva is solidifying into reality, its lines hardening, rehanging themselves according to the laws of gravity. I stretch out my hand on the building wall; the marble feels reassuringly cool.

I shiver, as a bitter current of wind swirls up through the great chasms between the office buildings. I go to lift my collar, but find I'm no longer wearing my old jacket; instead I'm dressed in an expensive wool business coat. I slide my fingers along the soft fabric, revelling in the feeling for a moment. I can't remember the last time I wore anything brand new.

'Oi, Citi boy.'

I spin around. Lola, dressed in understated Citiwear, stands a couple metres away, her deck tight in hand as she taps in data. We are the ultimate urban drone couple. I smile. She's spun us up another couple of tight Altforms, all right.

Lola jerks her head towards the lobby. 'We're here. Just running a card entry breaker through to the Associates. Need a little extra help to get ourselves through the door scanner.'

I glance over her shoulder as her deck strobes, codes

pulsing through the Drop. After a few seconds, Lola grins. 'Good to go. Shall we, Mr Griffin?'

I do a mock flourishy bow. 'After you, Signorina Rossi.'

Together we walk towards the lobby. As soon as we step through the entrance, a flat-eyed blond guard directs us to join the line for the entry scanner. My pulse quickens. It's a full body job.

Lola nudges me. 'Scanner bypass coming up. Just keep walking.'

Trying to keep my walk smooth and easy, I catch a flicker of movement on Lola's deck and suddenly the scanner dissolves and in a few seconds we emerge on the *other* side of the machine. Lola permits herself a tight smile as we move forward through the white lobby.

'Nicely done, Associates . . . and now as far as security is concerned, we're a couple of low-level traders from the Mumbai sister complex.'

Sliding my hands in my pockets I fall into step alongside Lola and it strikes me how little I really know about her. I mean, today is the first time I've ever been with her in the Drop proper. A girl from round my way functioning at this level, outsourcing herself on a global scale. It's incredible. I wonder what else I don't know about her, about Tais too.

'Anthony, concentrate.'

115

My head snaps up. 'I am.'

Lola regards me with a cool eye. 'I know that look, mate. *Dreaming.*'

I shake my head. 'No, I'm all here.'

Lola glances around the lobby. 'Now to find where they hide the vault. Might take a few minutes.'

I point inside an empty elevator. 'Let's get out of sight.'

Lola follows me inside and I press *Close Door* on the illuminated panel, holding the button locked down while Lola makes a rapid succession of keystrokes. She glances up. 'Time for a little diversion.'

'What's that mean?'

Lola smiles. 'As of four seconds ago a group of Debtbelt kids started up the sequence – a beautifully engineered virus dreamed up this afternoon by Han, a twelve-year-old physics geek from Shanghai – which is attacking the custodial commands for this building's security systems. And in about ten seconds' time it'll be followed by a command devised by my buddy Gabe in Baltimore. The command will pulse into the building's fabric – tricking each of its three separate alarm systems into thinking that the other two are still working.' Lola taps her deck. 'After that we wait another five seconds before the corporation's main alarm systems will detect the building is compromised. And that hopefully will trigger a code red.'

'What will that do?'

'Internal bots will activate a bunch of external security measures –which means they'll be looking *outside* when I'm already in. They're going to be way too busy to stop me from hacking into the internal architecture plans.'

'You sure?'

'Yeah. It'll be all over in nanoseconds. The security system will run a sweep, work out there's no danger and drop the code red. The complex would lose too much money if they closed the place down for any longer.'

Lola bends over her deck and after a brief pause her eyes light up. 'Genius.'

I peer over her shoulder, watch as a detailed architectural plan loads onscreen.

'It's on floor 379. Take us up, Anthony.'

I punch in the numbers and the elevator begins its ascent.

'This is where Star Holdings' records are kept, right?'

Lola curls her lip. 'Right – and it'll be the most guarded place in the whole building, especially just after an alarm. So let's take it slow when we get there.'

In a few seconds the lift comes to a halt, its doors sliding open on a platform, lined by a railing, that leads out on to an endless blank white space. I peer out and my stomach drops. I can't even work out how high up we are, it's like we're perched on the edge of an abyss.

I step towards the platform. 'Out here, right?'

Lola holds up her hand. 'Wait! Throw something outside first.'

'Like what?'

'Anything.'

Reaching into my pocket, I pull out a stick of gum and toss it on to the platform. Five laser points converge on it immediately, destroying it in a burst of energy.

Lola whistles. 'Shit. There must be a separate alarm system for the vault. We better pray the second sequence can crack through this.'

Squinting at the slip of paper the Teller gave me, Lola inputs a new line of data. Then she breathes a sigh of relief.

'OK, I think we're good. Try another stick of gum.'

Tapping out a fresh piece, I flick it out into the blank. And this time the gum spins outwards, no lasers, no smoke. But something's wrong. The gum isn't falling, it's spiralling outwards in a horizontal line.

'What the . . . ?'

Lola stares at it in dismay. 'Ah no. Zero gravity.' She shakes her head. 'There's no way I can go up in that and operate the deck at the same time.'

118

'Then I'll do it.'

She looks at me, doubtfully. 'You sure? Zero G is mental.'

'Just tell me what to do.' My stomach churns fresh acid as I peer over the side of the platform.

'It's all about moving slow. Even the tiniest overstretch will send you spinning round . . .'

I nod. 'OK. But where am I headed?'

Lola glances at her deck. 'Basically you've got to step off the platform and head two degrees north to begin with . . . I'll tell you the next move once you're on your way.'

I glance at her. 'You sure about this?'

'No.'

I swallow. 'Great.'

Lola shakes her head. 'You're right, it's too dangerous.'

I ram the gum packet back into my pocket. 'We can't blow a chance like this.'

And before I can change my mind I step out on to the platform, grab the railing and use it to drag myself to the end of the walkway. And then, heart in mouth, I force myself to let go. It's the weirdest sensation in the world. As I leave the railing, my arms fly outwards, ready for the drop, but instead my body glides forward, hovering thousands of metres above the ground. I glance to the side, at the white walls curving around me, coming together in the roof at an impossibly distant point – and suddenly panic bulges in my belly, wraps itself around my throat. I grapple the invisible air and the momentum hurls me into an endless forward somersault, my body rolling over and over, my arms and legs flailing in the void.

And then I hear Lola's voice in my ear. 'You've got to relax your body. Go completely still or you'll never come out of the spin.'

Gritting my teeth, I *make* my body be still. It goes against everything I *want* to do, but I know she's right. Rotating in the endless void, I order my muscles to go limp . . . and after a long, spiralling, sickening spin, I finally come to a stop and I'm still again, face down, a tiny dot in the vast chamber.

'Nicely done.' In this void air, Lola's voice sounds like she's five hundred miles away and a soft whisper in my brain simultaneously. 'Now head left, Anthony. Directions say Zone J. See the letters on the wall there?'

Blowing out a breath, I execute a series of small incremental turns towards the left.

After what feels like hours of creeping forward, with four different direction changes, Lola finally asks me to stop.

'Right. I've just activated the lock for the individual

account. Can you see anything?'

I rotate slowly, searching the space around me. And then, a few body lengths away, a small metal box suddenly materialises, hovering in space in just the kind of way that boxes don't. I roll my eyes. This place could mess your head up big time if you let it.

'I'm making my way over now.'

Wading through the zero gravity, I reach for the box, but I must be moving too fast and I lose control again, falling into another gut-wrenching extended roll. Tightening my throat against the vomit rising in my belly, I will myself to be still once more until I come to a hanging, lifeless stop. And then, my forehead dripping sweat, I gingerly reverse until I'm floating directly in front of the safe.

'You there yet?'

'Yes. Do I open it?'

'Think so. Should be unlocked.'

I reach for the handle and swing the box door outwards. It opens easily to the touch and gazing inside I see a small chamber, with a shelf running from wall to wall. On this lies a hexagonal hologram disc, roughly the size of my thumbnail.

'I see it, Lola! A disc.'

I start to reach forward.

She cuts me off. 'Wait up. We've got to time this right. I want to trick the system into thinking nothing is missing. So you need to pick it up the exact moment I do my thing down here.'

'What thing?'

'I'm gonna try and cover our tracks by executing a tiny shift in the vault's memory. Gabe says he can erase three seconds for us, and so if you can pull out the disc in that time, it'll be like it never happened. You good for that?'

'Think so.'

'You sure?'

I move my hand as close to the shelf as I can. 'Tell me when.'

'Now!'

I snatch at the disc. My fingers close around the hologram chip and I jerk my hand back, but I move too fast and I slam the base of my thumb against the edge of the box, sending the disc flying out of my grasp. I scream at myself to keep calm, to move my arm out real slow as I reach for it. But it ain't easy keeping calm, I'm so angry with myself – I've blown the three seconds big time. Suddenly from below comes a pulsing red core, a deep wailing alarm.

Lola's panicky voice is in my ear. 'What are you doing?'

'Hold on. Nearly got it . . .'

My fingers tighten so, so gently around the disc.

'Anthony? I'm pulling us out!'

My fist curls around the plastic. 'I've got it!'

Lola screams, 'Now!'

For a second I stare at the endless white vault around me, at the swirling mesh of lasers closing in. And then my stomach lurches, my body shrinks as the walls bend inwards, intense pressure filling my skull as I whip backwards. And then the vault's gates snap past me as I fall; the building a mass of collapsing debris flying through the air.

It's like I'm falling for ever. On and on and on and then a searing flash of pain jolts through my temple and suddenly I can feel grass tickling my face as I crash on to the earth. Where am I? This isn't the Drop. This isn't Lola's bedroom either. It's kind of familiar, but I can't remember why.

I stagger to my feet. The grass is chest high, slicing a pattern of fine cuts across my arms as I plunge forward until I crash into a clearing in the heart of the wood. Now I know where I am. I've been coming here since I was little. Grandad brought me first, and then I brought Tais. Yeah, I know where I am – I'm deep in the past, in a secret place only me and her shared. Without stopping for breath, I throw myself down on the ground, and then, with the grass and trees reaching over me, and birds and bugs rising and falling all around, I stare up at the blue and let the weight of the sky press me into the earth.

Sometimes Tais and me used to play these stupid games; we used to act like we weren't together. Once I blanked her for two weeks, can't even remember why. And then she blanked me back for a month. I was so desperate, man. I started working out in the back yard, trying to fix up, *build* up. Every day I set my alarm for six a.m. I was running up and down the garden; press-ups, curls, squats. I even carried a sack of coal on my back up and down. Old school, y'get me? Two raw eggs, honey and milk, I was drinking. The old way, the hard way. Rocky style. All the neighbours looking at me over their breakfast coffee, but I din't care. All I wanted was to get her back.

And that's all I want now. Tais was thrown from a walkway and for what? For some Betta guy to make a fast buck. The idiots and the scum they rise to the top but I won't let my girl be written off as another bad trade. I squeeze my eyes shut. And when you pray for real it's like a laser shooting out from your chest. It cuts out through your ribs, up, upward through the clouds and the sky and the atmosphere, all the way to heaven. A real prayer burns like a bitch.

124

'Anthony, wake up!'

My eyes snap open. In the bedroom, Lola is leaning over me, her vivid green eyes burning into mine.

'Say something.'

'S'thing.'

Lola laughs once, a high hysterical trill – and then collapses sideways on to her pillow and for a long minute we both lie like dead things, staring up at a bunch of fluorescent stars on her bedroom ceiling, y'know, that she probably stuck up there when she was a kid.

After a while I drag myself upright. A flash of pain shoots through my neck. 'I din't make the three seconds, Lola. I'm sorry.'

She swings her legs over the side of the bed, dropping her head into her hands. 'I know. That's why I pulled us out so fast. You still in one piece?'

'No.'

Lola sighs. 'We'd better not do that again in a hurry or we'll mess our heads up for good.' She pokes me. 'You still got the chip tho'?'

I open my hand. I've been holding it so tight it's cut a hexagonal mark into my palm.

Lola steadies herself and, reaching for her deck, slowly inserts it into the reader. 'We'll have to break this to get the data. I'll ask Han to do it.'

'Can we trust him?'

She presses her temple with her fingers. 'Yeh, he doesn't know what it's for. I'm keeping him out of all that. Plus, I . . . just ain't got the strength right now.' Lola leans back against the bed again. 'Sorry, Anthony. I can't even talk . . . I've got to rest up.'

I crouch beside her. 'You've been inside way too much these past two days.'

To my amazement, Lola's eyelids are already flickering. She is really wiped out.

I check the time. 'How long do you reckon Han will need?'

'Few hours . . . I'll buzz you when he . . . gets back . . . to me.'

'Promise?'

'Yeah.' Lola's eyes roll back in her head. 'You fine to . . . get home?'

'Sure.'

I stand up, slowly. My legs are still numb, clumsy. When I reach the door, I glance back at Lola.

'We did good, right?'

But she's already out. For a long moment I stare down at her face. The Teller is right, she does look young. Funny how I never noticed it before.

Turning the key in my front door, I stand in the hallway for a moment, reorienting myself. I can hear the radio and someone banging pots in the kitchen. That can only mean one thing. *Mom's home.* I take a couple deep breaths in the hallway, straighten my shoulders. We don't cross over much these days.

Heading down the hallway I stop just short of the kitchen and lean against the doorframe, watching my mom like some kind of junior psycho killer. She's sitting at the kitchen table, still dressed in her work clothes and crumbling crusts to feed the birds. I watch the way she tears the bread with her fingers. She's tense, but she's trying to hide it. She's trying to pretend her way back into our old life. All she wants is for us to get back to normality.

Some kind of normality. It's her new favourite phrase, y'know, on the phone to friends.

Suddenly she turns. 'Anthony, is that you?'

I give a little wave. 'Yeah.'

Her face brightens. 'Are you hungry?'

'Sure.'

After that crash from the Drop I feel like I never want to eat again, but Mom gets so wired after Stella has a meltdown. Sometimes Stel won't talk to her for days. Pulling myself away from the door, I pad over to the oven and lift the lid off a pan. I don't even know what I'm looking at. Mom is so hyper she's created a new form of life. Take a burger. Jump on it. Rest it in a pool of old chip oil. Fry until blacker than a witch's tit. Jump on it again. Cover in ketchup. Leave it to cool into set concrete in a pan. Mmmmm.

'There's beans too if you want them,' she says.

'Nah, this is cool,' I reply, forking it on to a plate.

From the garden comes a noise and a kind of screechy, wild flapping of wings. I turn to look. A bird has messed up his landing from the top of the wall on to the bird feeder and as I watch, he crashes into a water bowl. A kamikaze bird. He looks so furious, feathers all fluffed up in a ball, that I burst out laughing. I stare for a long moment more before dropping the lid on the pan and when I turn, I catch this flash of relief on my mom's face and I know it's there because I'm laughing at a *normal* thing, the bird, and that means she thinks I'm getting better, that I'm dealing with what happened to Tais. It's only a flash of a look, but it means all this, believe me.

I frown. 'I'm kind of behind with my revision. Do you mind if I go to my room to eat?'

Mom's fingers tighten around a hunk of bread. 'Of course. Thanks for dealing with Stella today.'

'No problem.' I cross the kitchen.

She smacks herself lightly on the forehead. 'Oh, I forgot. How did your exam go?'

'Good.'

Mom nods, puts a smile on her face, in her voice. *'That's good, then.'*

I run upstairs with that smile burned into my chest. People should only smile when they're happy. Otherwise, the other thing, the fake smile, it's just a killer. It's way worse than no smile because you know it's false and the other person knows it's false and you both know you both know this. And plus the one who gets false-smiled-at understands for sure when it happens that the other person thinks they're mental or lower than them. I blame *Friends*, man. Remember that show? Rachel, Monica, Chandler, Joey, Phoebe and Ross. They started it. OK,

Phoebe not so much. And now everyone does it, even my mom.

She's not sad though, not really. If you can get her going, if you can get her laughing, you're in business – you can make her laugh so hard her eyes crinkle up into tiny slits. I went through her account once, found this forum thread she'd posted. I mean, she's gone through a lot, especially with my dad leaving and all. But the thing is, it was like he was gone even when he was with us. And now it's just me left, the boy faking being a man. Jokes, right?

Angel from heaven? No pressure there, Mom.

And now I'm up in my room and it's late; my deck flashes 12.50. I'm stretched out on the bed and it's so good to be alone for a while, safe. No one ever comes in my room, not even Mom. I think she thinks I'm watching porn. *I'm at that age.* It's healthy. Although I've got to tell you, it kind of freaks me out sometimes, porn, y'know the way the camera, the way it zooms in on everything and I can't tell what bit belongs to who.

Night-time is mine. For a long while now I've had to wait till everyone goes to bed before I can let myself chill out. But once it's quiet and the last flush, the last creak, the last step is over and done – the house feels different then and I can think. I used to sneak down to the kitchen

Topic: It's getting better   POST REPLY   NEW TOPIC

Author	Message	Prev >> Next

J_G49

PROFILE

posted: June 01 @ 11.30 pm

she went from a sweet two year old, to like a demon had possessed her and was pulling us all inwards. we never slept for four years i was in a deep dark hole pulled in so many different directions i should have known and seen the signs you have all these hopes and dreams and now your child may never have friends, marry, oh the idea of her being lonely, i couldn't get out of bed if i believed that. But that gave me the courage to get up and fight this invisible enemy that comes in and takes your child. it's ok to grieve about it. why did this happen? I've got to keep loving her and talking to her til she calms. Anthony is like an angel from heaven with her. i'm better now

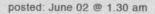
SUBMIT

Back to top

AlexR

posted: June 02 @ 1.30 am

All we can do is keep going. Thank you so much for sharing this words like this keep me going when i think i cant take it anymore.

sometimes and cook curries, real hot ones. And cakes too, yoghurt ones. And I always wanted to be a biochemist, a psychologist, a zoologist. I wanted to do something good in the world. And it's so weird because I can remember how I used to be and now all I do is watch myself smash myself into pieces.

And it's like I'm in a car crash, all slow and beautiful. Metal, plastic, glass – splintering, shattering, collapsing in on me, crushing me. And sometimes I feel so calm and peaceful – like all I want is to be folded up inside, hidden, small – and then at other times I fight it like a snarling dog. And I don't know which one of the me's is me any more.

My IQ is off the scale. I'm not bragging. I'm smart. If I get my grades I'm going places, I'm good. I see a problem and my mind opens it out and works out an answer clear. But right now all I want is sleep. I tell you, I'd trade in my stupid supersize me brain for a few hours of sweet sleep. But I can't do it. I close my eyes, I breathe, I *order* myself to relax, but all I've got is my head looping, endlessly replaying the Drop, Moskva Citi, the Teller's face, his clear amber eyes weighing me. Who is he, really? Someone on the inside, like a financier or a hedge-fund manager . . . or maybe he's something more radical, like a journalist or a spy? How did I get mixed up in all of this?

Sliding off my bed, I cross to the window. The moon, she's slanting over the roofs; catching the walls, the bricks, the branches of the trees, the fences, the gates – and everywhere she catches them different. Some places are dipped in silver but others trap her light in great ragged pits of secret black. Night places, dark places that don't seem to ever get any light, not even in a full moon. You know the ones, right?

I spread my fingers on the windowpane. I've lost normal. It's like I've been knocked two degrees sideways and I'm seeing life fresh new. I see us and the world like crystal, as if I'm looking down from outer space with all the lies like clouds blown clear away, and the shape of how we live laid out bare like countries below.

It's all Tais' fault. I'd give anything to cross back to the old country but I can't. Not now, not never. And it was the hospital when I started to go mad because that's where I started to notice that nobody ever shut up. What Tais needed was for people to come forward to the feds, to tell the truth, but all anyone ever did was talk nonsense. They'd gather around in the lobby of the hospital, on the street outside and they'd talk, talk about gangs, about society, about how terrible it all was. And then some of them they'd come to her bedside and call her name and cry.

And they all said the same words, repeated the same stories, cried the tears of despair . . . In the early days they did that, before they stopped coming, that is. In the end they made me feel sick to my stomach, I just wanted them to shut up because in the end they were just talking to make themselves feel better, they din't mean it. And do you know why humans talk so much? It's for protection. We use words as a shield because talking about things blocks out bad images and it cancels things we want to forget. Verbal overshadowing, it's called. I guess we first started doing it around the jungle fire, in a desperate bid to keep away the terror of the jungle night, and we ain't never quit since.

And if you don't believe me, then do a little experiment on yourself – watch a slasher movie, a real gore-fest, *alone*. And then observe as you get more and more freaked out, yeah? Before you know it, you'll be checking all the windows and the doors in the house and your heart will be climbing into your mouth at every creak in the floorboards, right? And why? Because you've got no one to talk it over with, to anaesthetise the bad images with words.

And I reckon if there was an alien in space and he came close to earth and listened in for a few minutes, he'd be amazed at this small blue-green planet and how it's swamped by great rivers of messages and Tweets and movies and virts . . . and I think he'd wonder what it was we were trying to cover up with our endless, endless talk. What a species. I mean, *c'mon*.

I mean, why do you think

not for even
one second,

do I ever, ever

shut up?

I wake with a start, my deck vibrating on the pillow beside me. Flinging out a hand, I hit the connect button and Lola's pale, tired face flickers on to the screen.

I rub my eyes. 'Thought you were sleeping.'

'Han cracked the disc.'

'What did he find?'

'A name.'

'We got a name? An actual name?'

'Yeah. The man who underwrote the Inspire takeover for Star Holdings is called César Desai. He holds an Indian passport but there's some Colombian family history there too.'

I swing my legs over the side of the bed. 'This is so cool—'

'Uh-huh.'

I frown. There's something wrong with her voice. It's too flat.

'What's up?'

'That's it. We can't go any further.'

'What d'you mean?'

'Dead end. No matter what search Han ran, all he ever got was the name and the passport before the firewall came down. We can't locate him.'

'But I thought the Teller said the name in the Geneva vault had to be legit . . . that there had to be a real person and address to back it up.'

Her voice drops. 'Yeah well that's the thing. This César guy does have an address, but Han can't access it. He's tried everything, me too, but it's impossible.'

'Why?'

'Because Inspire is registered as an offshore ID in Bermuda – and so is Desai. And that only means one thing.'

'What?'

'Star Holdings aren't the company who hired the Betta to do a hack for them. They *are* the Betta. '

The back of my neck prickles. 'How do you know?'

'Different pirates own different offshores. The Betta trade through Bermuda, they kicked everyone else out after the crash . . . everybody working the Drop knows it.'

I slam my hand down on the bed. 'So we went through all of that for nothing?'

'I – I – don't know.'

'Well, what if we contacted the Teller again?'

Lola shrugs. 'He's not responding to my messages. I've been trying for hours. So . . . it looks like we're on our own from here on in.'

I rise from the bed, a cold shiver running through my body as my bare feet touch the floor.

'So what now?'

'I don't know.'

'What do you mean? We can't just stop . . . we're getting close—'

'To the *Betta*, Anthony. *Think*. Round here they're mostly street level, but a major company like Star Holdings, that's way too high-level. We can't risk going anywhere near them.'

I can feel the blood rushing to my face. 'You're just like all the others.'

'What's that supposed to mean?'

'The feds, school, my mom . . . you all just want me to forget it ever happened.'

She shakes her head. 'That's not true.'

My heart starts to pound, fast. 'Face it Lola, you want

all of this to go away – I bet you're glad it's the Betta so you can back out.'

Her face freezes. 'I ain't gonna die because of your guilt.'

My voice is shaking. 'Like all the others you are. You'll be telling me to move on, to *let myself grieve* in a minute. You don't care about her at all.'

Lola gasps; a swoosh, a suck, a vacuum. The second, the nanosecond the words come out I want to dive after them, yeah, drag them back inside me. But it's too late.

Lola's voice drops to a hiss. 'The way you act, like it's just you who hurts. Not everyone's like you . . . I . . . can't let it get to me like you, otherwise . . .'

'What?'

'I just – can't. I know it'd eat me alive, like it's doing to you.' Suddenly she jerks her hand over her eyes.

I stare at the screen in dismay, all my anger dissolving. I can't believe I've made Lola Rossi cry. It's impossible. I draw in a ragged breath. 'Ah, come on. I didn't mean it. I'm sorry, OK?'

Head bowed, she sits silent.

I try again. 'You're the only one I trust.'

Lola glares up at me. 'Why? You just said I'm a fake.'

'I was stupid. I din't mean it.'

Suddenly the screen flickers and when it steadies once

more, Lola's face is blank, and her voice is flat again, under control.

'You can't ask me to take on the Betta. It's too much.'

We stare at each other a long moment. I swallow. 'You're right . . . you've done enough already.'

She reaches out her hand, pressing her fingertips to the screen. 'It's too much to ask.'

'I know.'

'I'm so sorry, Anthony.'

'It's OK. Honest.' I reach up to disconnect.

'Wait!' Lola's face blurs. Suddenly tears are streaming down her cheeks again. 'What are you going to do now, you freak? I can't lose you too.'

I lean forward. 'I've got to go now.'

'Stop it. You're scaring me!'

I look at her and it's true she looks scared; I mean she looks *really* scared, like I'm some crazy man. I don't want her to be frightened like this. I've got to reassure her.

'What's the matter? It's me . . . Anthony.'

And suddenly this feeling of wanting to escape sweeps over me. All I want is to leave this whole mess behind, blow it into dust.

'Let's run away. I can't stand it here no more.'

She frowns. 'What?'

'I'm gonna die if I stay any longer.'

'What are you talking about?'

'Just let's go away, *now*.'

Lola's voice cracks. 'I can't just leave. We're in the middle of our exams, remember?'

'I've only got one left. And anyway I blew Biology, remember? I don't care about uni no more. Please, please . . . come with me.'

'But where?'

'Abroad. Anywhere.'

'But—'

'But *what*? We could like . . . work the Drop together and live on the cash for months.'

Lola wipes her eyes with the back of her hand, cracks a smile. 'It could be huge.'

'Two fingers up to all the triple A's on their gap year.'

'We'll be a movement.'

'An army. Of two.'

Lola's face splits into a wide grin. 'We'll be famous.'

'We'll be so massive famous.'

We both burst out laughing – and then the stupid smile freezes on my face as I realise what Lola's doing. She's trying to calm me down. She doesn't mean a word of what she's saying. She's making jokes with me to calm me down like I'M CRAZY AND SHE'S NOT. This makes me even madder than before. Balling my hand into a fist I punch my bedroom wall before doubling over in silent pain, biting back the tears. (It's never a good plan to punch a wall by the way, you always come off the loser.) When I finally turn to the screen again, Lola is staring at me intently.

'Anthony, you've got to get some help. You're not OK.'

'But you're OK, yeah?'

I can't talk like this no more. I reach up and rip the power cable out of my deck; the screen dies in my hands. I can't be like this no more. Even Lola's on the other side.

For a moment I gaze around my room, revolving a new plan of action in my mind. If the Teller doesn't contact me again, there's only one thing I can think to do, only one person to turn to if I want to get to the Betta. I glance at the clock. 2.50. He'll still be up. It's Friday night. I'd bet my last credit he'll be at Sapphire's. I reach up for my old denim jacket.

Creeping out of my room, I close the door softly behind me, but then I pause for a moment on the landing. Stella's light is still on. Sometimes she doesn't sleep for days on end. I stand there and I know I should check on her, but in truth I don't want to. I'm geared up, adrenaline pumping through my veins.

'I can hear your breathing, you know.' Stella's high voice comes from inside her room.

Hell, I have to go in now. Turning the handle I push her door open a few centimetres. Stella is sitting at her desk.

I try a smile. 'Hey! What you up to?'

She shrugs. 'Journal.'

It used to be *no* eye contact for days and days after something like today, but Stella's working on it. She's working on herself. But I can see she's made herself ultra neutral, she must've taken two Ritalin tablets. She's flattened herself out. It's either that or be angry, she says. Very, very angry. People think she's being rude, ignoring them. But she's not, she's just trying to be more normal. More like other people. Imagine all that going on inside you and you're eleven?

I take a couple paces into the room.

'Want to read it to me for a minute?'

She shakes her head.

'Go on, Stel, for *me*.'

She sighs, but then she begins to read out loud, the way she always does, a high sing-song burst of words with stresses in funny places.

'The Crow people's real name is the *Apsáalooke*. They are a Sioux tribe *and* come from the Yellowstone River valley. *Apsáalooke* was turned into French as *gens du corbeaux* meaning *people of the crows* but it actually means *children of the large-beaked bird*. After the Europeans came to America, the Crow Nation fought them, *but* they lost. They now live on a reservation in Montana.'

I raise an eyebrow. 'When did they move there?'

Stella taps her fingers on her desk. 'I don't know. I haven't researched that.'

'Well, I'm just asking is all.'

'This isn't about dates. It's about Crows.'

'OK. Sorry.'

'Hmm.'

Stella bends over her deck again. 'The Crow People believe that the Human People are incomplete and we need help from nature. And this help is called Medicine or Baaxpee and this is *power* and it is hidden inside the *land* and we can find it and use it but only if we are very gentle. And they *say* this is the point of life, to *maintain* the harmony of everything, of the Animal, *Plant* and Spirit People *who* are our family.'

I hold up my hand. 'What was that thing called again?'

Stella glances up. 'Which thing?'

'The one beginning with B.'

'Baaxpee?'

'Uh-huh.'

She flicks to another journal page, her eyes travelling down the text. 'Baaxpee is a spiritual power *and* it is for turning a person into an *adult* but only after they go through a lot of pain will they change and then *they* can be called Xapaaliia. And that means they are a warrior who cannot be *killed* by bullets.' She taps her teeth. 'Can I go back to my original story now?'

'Knock yourself out.'

I need to get moving, but I'm so happy my sister is talking that I lean back and let Stella's words flow over me. If I'm five minutes late then so be it.

Stella is reading again. 'And what's really interesting is the Crow People are not stuck in some clockwork universe where they don't have any *effect* on anything. The Crow People wind the world up every *morning* with special ceremonies *and* keep it ticking all day long to keep the world going. They don't own *lots* of things like we do, they only have one special thing, like a spear or a shield or a necklace that is like a part of themselves and this is the thing that means most to *them* in the world, and they call this special thing their *extension* object. Oh, and finally the Crow People say when you do something, you *should* burn yourself completely, like a good bonfire and leave no trace of yourself. *Just* ashes. The End.'

Tais. As Stella's voice dies away, her face rises before me. Vivid. What was her special ceremony? Nothing. A Junker. A Debtbelt girl. Nobody celebrated her and nobody avenged her when she got hurt. But I'm going to change all that. Right now. I zip my jacket up.

'Cheers Stel, that was cool.'

For the first time, she takes in my jacket. 'Are you going out somewhere?'

'Yeah. I'm going to meet a friend . . . in a club. Don't tell Mom, right?'

She shakes her head, scornful. 'Think I'm stupid?'

'No.'

'Are you going to dance?'

I frown. 'Dunno. Maybe.'

'You shouldn't, you know.'

'Why not? It's not dangerous down there . . .'

A sly look comes to her eyes. 'I know that. But you're a really bad dancer.'

I lunge forward, pretending to swat her on the head and Stella dives under the covers with a shriek of laughter.

But as I turn to leave the room, I catch a glimpse of my reflection in the wall mirror. Xapaaliia. A warrior who cannot be killed by bullets. Jokes, right?

I set out for the Sapphire Club. Even though it's late, it's still hot and the streets are kind of buzzy – feels like half the neighbourhood is still up and about and my heart rises as I stride along. I like the night the best. It's more honest somehow – city buildings with their blind windows, folk asleep in bus shelters, all drunk and full of big words.

Some twenty minutes later, I arrive, but I don't go into the club, not yet. For a while I stand in the shadows on the kerb opposite and check out the action. Sapphire's is a local legend, a sweaty old dive that's been here since back in the day; the exit lined with beefy bouncer guys and groups of nearly naked girls leaning against the wall, chattering like tropical birds. Meanwhile on the street, pimped-up cars cruise by in an endless line, their chrome spoilers gleaming in the lamplight, heavy bass lines spilling from the speakers inside.

And as I watch the girls I can see they're laughing and talking together, but all the while they're taking sneaky peeks at the cars going by because that's where the Betta boys are, cruising up and down the block. It's like a courtship ritual on a nature programme. I even recognise one or two of the girls, they're triple A's from the good side of town. I've seen them down at the mall a few times. But tonight they're slumming it, out for a thrill, mixing it up with us junkers and the gangster boys.

I slide out of my jacket. It's a sticky night, all right. It feels like trouble, it feels like business. But that's good because I'm here on business too. I'm on the hunt for Ali.

I cross the street, and as I near the roped-off entrance, an armour-plated jeep draws up to the kerb alongside me. Without thinking, I turn to stare as the passenger door opens. A young guy in a slim-kut iridescent suit slides out, ducking his head to protect his luminous orange quiff from the door rim. Stepping on to the sidewalk, he pulls up short.

'What you looking at?'

'Nothing.'

I can't take my eyes from his face. He reminds me of someone, but I can't think who.

A snarl spreads across his features, catching the scar that twists from his lip down to his chin.

'You callin' me nothing?'

Suddenly a girl behind me snatches up my hand, whispers in my ear. 'Let's go in, babe. The line's nearly gone.'

I turn in surprise as the girl's hand tightens around mine. The Betta boy's eyes flicker from my face to hers and suddenly he leans over, spits. 'Best listen to the girl.'

And with that he shoves past me along the street.

I turn to the girl. 'Thanks.'

She brushes her fringe out of her eyes. 'You're a friend of Tais', right?'

I nod. 'Yes.'

'Then a word to the wise. Don't stare. It winds people up.' And with that she lets go of my hand and struts back down the line.

Giving myself a mental shake, I walk up to the entrance booth. I've got to pull myself together. I'm acting like some kind of cop in a shit tube show. I mean, even that stupid detective Daniel Garcia would know better than to stand round street corners staring at Betta gangsters like a stuffed owl.

149

After I pay my money I clatter down the poky staircase and push through a set of double doors into the main hall. For a moment I stand at the threshold – as a great blast of sweaty heat from the crowd, the lights, the beat, rolls over me. I scan the room for Ali, starting at the left side, over by the foosball machines. And then my heart sinks. Max and a couple of triple A boys from my old school are standing in a tight group around the curved edge of the bar.

My eyes harden. Did I tell you how much I hate Max? I can't remember. He's the kid I slammed into in the testFrame booth yesterday morning, right? And just so you know, it ain't some casual hatred I've got for him. No, I detest his very core of being, right down to his molecular structure. Tais she always used to talk to him far too much. But it's more than that. Max is everything I'm trying to get away from. Him and his pri-mates with opposable digits and basic grunts. Knuckle-draggers in Ted Baker shirts they are. They all do Business or Marketing and their big dream is to be the office alpha male so they can swing around the desks, beating their pumped-up steroid chests. I mean, I ain't no angel, but those guys are the dark side of man. If I made a virt I'd crush Max with a car or an elevator during the opening titles in slo-mo ultra 3D. Totally.

Crossing the crowded room, I head for the opposite end of the bar and order a Coke. I can't get distracted by those bozos, my business is with Ali tonight. He's got to be around somewhere, I know for sure he does a lot of business down here at the weekend. And then, suddenly, there's a whisper in my ear. I freeze.

'Wun't you love to hack into that Max boy's university application, tell the truth for once?'

I turn around. Ali is right there, his eyes fixed on the group at the far end of the bar. I grin, following his gaze. 'I am white, male and loud. I do not have a lot of brains but what I do have is a lot of money. I know my place and it is at the top.'

Ali's eyes crinkle with laughter. 'Yeah. I want to study Economics or Nano-trading yet have always wanted to make a real difference to people's lives . . .'

I take a swig of my Coke. '. . . In my gap year, I will be not only be an intern for a major corporation but I will also be a volunteer in the favelas of Rio de Janeiro, where I will work in a youth centre with camera-friendly slum kids, who will brighten up my CV no end.'

Ali shakes his head with satisfaction. 'And I will bowl you over at interview in a way that a poor person never can. They may get better grades than me, but they still lack my insane levels of belief that I belong at the top.'

151

I grin. 'Plus I am good for the money. You know I'm not going to drop out due to lack of funds . . .'

'So . . . in summary . . . I am right for your course . . . because . . .'

We shout in unison, '. . . I'm worth it.'

Ali throws back his head and laughs. A long hearty laugh – and I laugh too cos it's a long time since me and him were like this.

He glances at me. 'So, who are you down here with?'

'No one.'

'Sharking around is it?'

I shrug.

He fake punches me on the shoulder. 'Well, it's good to see you lightening up, yeh?'

I lean forward. 'No, not really. The truth is I've come looking for . . . you.'

The smile dies on his lips.

'Why?'

'I need your help.'

He groans. 'No more, man.'

I drop my voice. 'I've got to trace someone in your . . . organisation. You're the only one I can ask.'

The scar on his mouth flares. 'You're joking, right?'

I stare into his face.

'No. I've just found out tonight it was a Betta who

ordered Tais dead. For real.'

Ali's jaw tightens. 'Who says?'

'I can't tell you.'

Ali shakes his head. 'Go home, Anthony.'

I jut my jaw out. 'You remember Tais, don't you?'

His head snaps around. 'What's that supposed to mean?'

But for once I don't back down.

'She was your friend too, right?' I swallow, *hard*, and for a long frozen moment we stare at each other, but we can't find any words, because we've let it all get too big now. And as we face off, suddenly the lights and beat die and the club falls into blackout followed a few moments later by a half-stifled scream from the dance floor. And then, close by, a gunshot rings out and the club *explodes* into a seething, terrified mass of bodies.

Ali grabs my shoulder.

'Quick. The back stairs.'

I follow him as best I can through the gasping, seething pit. Battling our way through the crush, we finally reach the narrow stairs at the rear of the bar, only to slam up against a whole bunch of people with the same idea. But Ali shoulder-charges his way through the throng, dragging me up behind him – until finally he rams his shoulder against a rusty fire-door – and shoves me out into a back alley.

153

Whirling around I swing wildly at him but he ducks and I overbalance. Staggering sideways, I try to swing again, but he's too quick for me, and the next thing I know I'm pressed flat up against the dirty alley wall, my cheek squished against the rough bricks.

'Anthony, you gotta grow up.'

I squirm under his arm. 'What happened to you, Ali? You used to hate bullies and now look at you. Lower than any of them.'

Ali spins me around, grabs me by my T-shirt and lifts his fist to strike.

'Go on, then!'

But for a long moment he just holds me there, judging me, judging what to do. And then he relaxes his grip.

'You got to let her go,' he mutters.

I hang my head. 'I can't. She won't let me be.'

Ali leans heavily against the wall. 'There's rules, Anthony. She broke 'em.'

I glare at him. 'So you're saying it's OK what they did?'

Ali slams his fist into his palm. 'Course it ain't. But it's just how it is, *business*. No more no less, ai'ght?'

'People don't die doing business.'

'Tais knew what the life was. She made a choice.'

'No she din't.' I jerk my thumb behind me. 'And Max and those idiots inside they've got everything.'

'It's the way it is.'

I push myself from the wall and we're face to face again before I know what I'm doing. 'I can't accept that. I've got hard information that it's a Betta leader that ordered the hit. Don't you want to help?'

Ali's face twists. 'You and your little clues, Anthony. You're a joke, man.'

I look him up and down. 'At least I haven't sold out like you.'

Suddenly I'm too mad to talk. What's the point? Diving under his arm, I start to jog back down the alleyway, heading for the front of the club. Ali calls from behind me.

'You've got to listen to me.'

I shake my head. 'No I don't.'

'Then you're on your own.'

I shrug. 'Tell me something new.'

As I reach the end of the alley I crouch down, checking for danger. The power cut is over; I can hear the dull thud of music again. The surge of panic has flattened down as fast as it broke. Still, there's a semi-circle of Betta, chains in hands, grouped near the ropes at the entrance to the club. I bite back the bitter choke in my throat. What am I doing here, coming for help? Ali, Lola, they're all the same in the end. Cowards. I'm so mad all I want to do is run into the middle of the Betta, challenge the whole lot of them.

I tense my body, ready to dive out on to the street, and that's when it comes – the blood-red Mustang, nosing down the street like a big old lazy shark. *The car I saw on the day of Tais' hit*. I can't believe what I'm seeing. After all these weeks of searching. Finally!

Ducking back into the alley, I stare as the Mustang pulls up into the shadows just beyond the club. As it slows, a figure steps out from under a shop awning, moving towards the car with quick strides. I can just make out the passenger window rolling down as the figure approaches the door. My chest tightens; a steel band contracting around my ribs. I've got to get closer.

Suddenly Ali's hand is on my shoulder, his voice low. 'Please, man. Go home. For *me*.'

I jerk my thumb towards the Mustang. 'Whose car is that?'

'Why don't you listen?'

I turn to him. 'Come on, Ali. It's the last thing I'm ever going to ask you.'

Reluctantly he glances down the street, his eyes widening as he sees the car.

'Don't know.'

'Liar.'

'I ain't lying.'

'Then it's safe for me to go over there?'

'No!' His hand tightens on my T-shirt.

But I jerk forward, ripping free of his grip and walking towards the car. When I get to within a few metres of the Mustang I bend down, pretending to tie my laces. But I'm still not close enough. The guy leaning through the window is completely blocking my view of the interior. He laughs, hitting his thigh with a slap – and steps back a pace or two, but I still can't see clearly. It's too dark. The Mustang's engine revs. I've got to do something. Whoever's in there ain't going to stick around for long.

Desperately, I throw myself forward in a fake trip that leaves me sprawling on the kerb down by the Mustang's front bumper. The guy standing at the window jerks back, surprised, and for a second I stare up into his face. Ah no, it's the same man as before, his orange quiff glinting in the street light above me.

His eyes narrow. 'You again? You're gonna get a kicking this time, for real.'

But I'm not looking at him, I'm twisting my neck to see into the car, but before I can catch a glimpse, the Betta guy kicks me in the gut. Pain explodes through me. I try to get up, but he kicks me again. I curl up like a worm, raising my knees to protect my stomach. Now his boot is on my neck. I freeze. Is he going to kick me in the head? Panic grips me. There's not going to be any Ali this time.

And then a voice comes from inside the car. 'Leave him be.'

'I'm just teaching him a little lesson.'

'I said, *leave it*. I don't want any trouble tonight.'

My man's eyes flicker, puzzled, but after a moment I feel the weight on my throat lift as he removes his boot from my windpipe. Taking my chance I pull myself upright, peering into the car. A woman sits in the passenger seat; graceful, one manicured hand resting on the doorframe. I look into her face; a cool, calculating mask, dominated by strange, yellow cat eyes.

She cocks her head, measuring me. I hold my breath, forcing my expression to stay neutral. Was she there at the time of Tais' hit? Will she remember me? And then her expression changes; a look of disdain, *disinterest* spreads across her features. This woman no more remembers me than she would a dog in the street. I'm too low. The silver bangles on her arm rattle as she claps her hands together.

'Out of here, Younger. Before you get hurt.'

The Mustang engine revs again and she glances at the Betta with the orange quiff. 'Four, tomorrow. Got that?'

He nods, the driver guns the engine and in seconds the Mustang disappears in a cloud of blue smoke. I quickly clamber to my feet and for a moment the Betta boy and me regard each other in silence.

He shakes his head. 'You a lucky dog, man.' And then suddenly he grabs me by my T-shirt. 'Listen, you . . . when was you ever properly scared?'

I stare into his eyes, say nothing.

'Not worry or stress, but proper *fear*?' His eyes harden. 'Cuz I look at you and I know that you believe, deep down, that whatever happens that you'll be ai'ght. Cuz you come from that world, where things turn out good.' A bitter curl twists his lip. 'But out here, brother, that's all over. Now get home 'fore I change my mind and give you the kickin' you surely deserve.'

And with that he turns on his heel and stalks back into the shadows. I don't need no second telling. I set off at a fast limp back down the street. And when I pass the alleyway, I don't even turn my head to see if Ali is still there. And I've never felt so alone in the whole of my life. Because he's wrong, I'm not from that world where things turn out good. Not any more, I ain't.

I don't know what happens next, not clear, but I know I walk for hours. Street after street after street; I lose myself in the steady pump of movement, almost till I can't feel my legs no more. I keep to the shadows, while above me the moon sails out from between the clouds, and she hangs so low, it's like I can almost see through her pale skin to her organs beneath.

And the further I walk, the stronger my animal senses turn; after a couple hours, my sharp ears are picking up the steady pump of heating vents, water trickling through pipes, the tick and rattle of electricity through buried wires. Up ahead of me, the city lies; a loose collection of lights, milky and blurred, but where I am it's deep dark. Not a soul on the streets, everyone is asleep like monkeys up in their apartment trees, safe from predators – and when they wake tomorrow it'll be like the forest waking up too, radios and the tube and breakfast-table grunts.

When finally I can't take another step I stagger into an all-night diner and fling myself down in a seat near the window. Oh man, all I want to do is not think, but my mind keeps on grinding on, desperately searching for a new plan of action.

Ordering a coffee, I cup my hands around the warm mug and then I stretch my legs out under the plastic table, staring through the smeary window as the pale pink of dawn tugs at the corner of the sky. What time is it? I take out my deck to check . . . and it's then I see the message.

TELLER: One-hour window. *You set the Drop destination.*

My pulse starts to race. Have I missed him? Heart in mouth, I check the time of the message. It came forty-five minutes ago. I've still got time, but sweat pricks at my palms. What am I going to do? I don't know anything about locations in the Drop, apart from some real low-level areas. But fifteen minutes is all I've got. Flicking through my deck Drop options, my eyes fall on a lurid pink neon sign. It'll have to do. I hit my *re>message*.

AGRIFFIN: *Meet me in the Park View Motel.*

In seconds a message flies back. Yes, he's still there!

TELLER: Hurry. 15 minutes only left on the jammer.

I glance around the greasy diner. There's nobody here except a couple of druggies by the counter, grinding their teeth in comedown. Even so, I change seats and hunker down low at a table at the rear, lining up a bunch of plastic ferns on the chipped tabletop in front of me for full camouflage. As I prepare to Drop, my face momentarily splits into a grin. Now I look like the biggest druggie of the lot. Lord Anthony and his grove of fern friends. Anyway, I ain't got time to care about appearances. Fishing my 'trodes out of my back pocket, I raise my visor to my eyes and jack in.

Sliding through a blur of grey and pink neon, I find myself standing in the lobby of a cheap motel chain. I peek through the window, almost expecting to see a flyover or a motorway outside, y'know the kind of view these places always have. But there's nothing like that out there, only a car wash across the street. I turn, scanning the lobby for the Teller.

There's a bunch of people milling around the place; it looks like there's some kind of convention going on, but nothing with any money behind it. Everybody's wearing suit trousers that are sort of shiny around the knees or they've got stains on their jacket lapels. This is the

Eurozone Drop for sure, strictly for losers.

And then I catch sight of the Teller; he's standing right by the front desk, a folded handkerchief delicately pressed to his nose. I quickly cross to his side.

'No bodyguard today?'

He raises an eyebrow. 'No need, for this dump. Nice choice, Anthony.'

'I was in a hurry.'

He jerks his head towards a corridor. 'Come, let's find somewhere more private.'

After trying a couple of locked doors, the Teller pushes his shoulder against the next door he comes to – a thin, plywood thing – and after a couple of shoves the door gives way and he falls forward into a crappy function room. I wrinkle my nose. It's like where my dad had his wedding reception, y'know with that kind of speckly carpet that you can't tell where the dropped Doritos end and the rug pattern begins . . . ? The Teller examines an armchair before placing one buttock cheek primly on the arm. He looks pretty out of place, I can tell you.

I sit down opposite him on a sofa. A shudder runs through my body – my limbs feel like wet newspaper after that walk, old, warped and heavy with rain.

The Teller clears his throat. 'So, what did you find out

in Geneva?'

'A name—'

He holds up a warning hand. 'Don't tell me who. I need not know.'

'It's no use anyhow.'

His eyes widen. 'Why not?'

'We can't locate him.'

'What do you mean?'

'No address. Lola ran every check she knows and came up with zero.'

'But there must be an address. By international law the vault deed has to contain a legitimate name and location.'

'Yeah well it did. Bermuda.'

His face falls. 'Ah. I see.'

'I – I tried to ask a Betta friend for help.'

'And he refused you?'

I nod.

The Teller sighs. 'Hardly surprising. Bermuda is serious business.'

I straighten. 'What goes on there? I mean I know it's a tax thing, but what does that mean exactly?'

His amber eyes meet mine. 'Bermuda is much, much more than a tax haven; it's a place where the super rich operate. Did you know they now own sixty per cent of the globe's entire wealth? One per cent of one per cent, they function with a completely different set of rules from the rest of us. It is maybe like quantum physics . . .'

'I don't get it.'

A smile touches his lips. 'Well, you know that when you get down to the level of the atom in quantum physics, the normal rules break down and you have to work with a completely new set of parameters?'

I nod.

'And if the old laws break down at this Quantum Level, suddenly things don't function like they do in the normal world. You cannot tell if an atom is a wave or a particle because actually it is both, *simultaneously*. It is two *completely* different things at the same time, you understand?'

I shrug. 'Kind of.'

'Well, so it is with these elites and their money. You cannot ever tell where or what form their money will take. One minute they are using it to prop up a bad bank, then they're taking over a football club, then they're fuelling a housing bubble, then they're shorting a currency, then they're moving billions offshore to avoid tax. And they do this all at the same time and all totally legally. They run rings around the world.'

'Then why doesn't someone stop them?'

He sighs. 'Nobody knows how. They are very clever . . .

and as a species we are very bad at big numbers.'

I glance at the time. We've only got seven minutes before the Drop window closes, but the Teller doesn't seem to care right now. He traces an urgent pattern on his knee.

'I show you. How long is a million seconds?'

I shrug. 'Look, could we get on to Tais, I want to know if there's any other way—'

He leans forward, urgent. 'Try.'

Frowning, I attempt the maths in my head. 'A month?'

His mouth folds into a smile. 'No. Twelve days.'

'Er, OK.'

'Now try with a billion.'

'Ah, look, I dunno.'

'*Try.*'

'Six months?'

'Thirty-two years.'

I whistle. 'Oh.'

'You see? We're no good at it. Our brains are not hardwired for calculating big numbers or risk and yet we keep marching on as if we're some kind of super species. It's like we are blind. We need to learn to see ourselves as we really *are* if we're ever going to get out of this mess.'

I glance at the time again. Now only five minutes left. I lean forward.

'Sir, we've only got a short time left . . . is there

anything you can do to help me locate this man in Bermuda . . . ?'

The Teller's eyes meet mine. 'And what if there is? He will just be replaced by another and another and another. Capitalism is a virus. Its only motivation is to replicate.'

I slam my hands down on my knees. '. . . Because Tais is worth more than money!'

He sighs. 'You don't know what you ask me. I take a great risk in meeting you like this. If I do any more I will surely be detected. You wish for another death on your conscience?'

'No!'

'Because that is what she is, right? This friend of yours. You are eaten up with guilt because you are alive and it is her lying in the hospital bed.'

My hand moves towards my deck. 'Look, sorry I asked for help.'

I start to rise to my feet, but the Teller stands up, lays his hand upon my shoulder.

'You don't know what you're doing.'

'So? That's my problem, not yours.'

His fingers tighten on my jacket. 'How good a friend is your Betta contact?'

'He used to be my best friend. Now I don't know.'

The Teller stares at the carpet, eyes narrowed. 'If you

can bring him onboard there is maybe something I can do . . . create for you a temporary high-level Altform hacker ID.'

'And what good will that do?'

'If your friend introduces you to his Betta contacts as a new Debtbelt hacker, a replacement for Tais . . . for sure it will bring you closer to the man you want.'

'But how could that ever work? As soon as any Betta met me in the Drop they'd know I was a fake.'

He frowns. 'The Altform I can spin will give you good enough cover for a few meetings.'

I blow out my cheeks. 'But this man, he'd never meet directly with me, would he?'

'For sure, he'd run some checks first, but you'd be surprised with these guys. They still like to recruit people face to face; there are just too many traps and fakes in the Drop . . . And my hunch is that although his address is concealed in Bermuda, he might physically be closer than you think.'

I shake my head. 'He's going to take one look at me and kill me on the spot.'

The Teller nods, gravely. 'Yes, probably. But you asked for my help. And so I offer you the Altform. But my true advice is to make your peace with the girl and let this go.'

I shake my head, slowly. 'I can't.'

He sighs. 'Then take my Altform ID. I will send it in code.' He glances at a slim platinum watch on his left wrist. 'And now we must go. We have only seconds left.'

I reach for the decompression key on my deck. 'Will I see you again?'

'I don't know if that will be possible. But I wish you good luck. For what it's worth . . . I – I think Tais was worth more than money too.'

For a long moment he stares at me, and then takes a step backwards as the lines of the function room begin to twist and bend, the pink neon turning yellow, then silver, then grey . . .

27, 28, 29, 30 . . .

I'm falling, falling . . . and then suddenly it's hot, hot summer, and I'm lying up in Tais' room. We're playing Monopoly, the old-fashioned way, with the board and everything. I love playing Monopoly with Tais; she always cracks me up because she gets so *mad* when she has to pay me out any money. You should see her face when she lands on a bunch of my hotels. But I never let on it cracks me up cos then she'd try to hide it and I like it so much when her eyes go all flashy and she does this thing with her chin, sort of juts it out. You never saw such a chin.

The windows are wide open and Tais is wearing like a little T-shirt and shorts and all of a sudden her dad shows up in the doorway and tells her to go to the shops for him. She doesn't answer him though and so he asks her again but still she doesn't answer, she kind of makes out as if she hasn't heard him, even though he's there, right there. I don't know what to do, I'm staring down at the board, trying to be invisible and then her dad, he makes a movement. I don't even know what he does, something with his hand, a kind of a clenched fist, but not even that big, just a tightening, a whitening of his fingers. I look up into his face and see him staring at her and I know that if I wasn't there that fist would've been for real, it would have been for Tais or for her little sister. I just know it.

And in that moment I understood I could never say anything to Tais, *ever* about what just happened. Because some things you can't share. And I remember it made me feel so sad, how close you can be to someone and how far away, all at the same time.

And then the room tips and I start to slide. Desperately I grab at the bed sheets, but it's no good, I'm falling again . . .

The grey walls of the diner coalesce about me once more

and I open my eyes with a start. I'm back at the table, slumped down low in the orange plastic chair behind my little row of plastic ferns. I sit, stunned, breathing in, breathing out, waiting for the vertigo to pass.

And you know, I want to set the record straight, I ain't doing what I'm doing out of guilt. I'm not sentimental like that. Tais knew what she was doing was wrong. She got mixed up with a bad crowd. But the way I see it is at least she knew who she was and what she was doing it for. She was hacking for the Betta to get her little sister out of the house, to build a new life for them far away from her old man.

And when someone is in a coma, all you want them to do is wake up. I sat in the hospital with Tais for hours, staring at her, waiting for her eyes to open, for her fingers to move. But people don't wake up like that, *snap*. No, when someone is in a coma, waking up is a really, really big deal and it goes through all these slow stages. And the doctors they call it *emerging*.

And I remember reading this woman's story of how she woke up from her coma. And she said what happened was as she lay there in that bed, she made a choice to live rather than die: she called it *making a contract with herself*. She decided she wasn't going to be a victim no more. And that's what I want, more than anything else. I want to take control, even if for only a minute, and make Tais' life mean something.

In the diner, I rise from the table and stretch my aching muscles as I peer out through the dirty window. It's full day now and I'm out in the open again. Glancing down at my deck, I watch as a long stream of code stacks up on the screen. My heart rate starts to climb. It's the Teller's Altform code. He's kept his end of the bargain. Now it's time to keep mine. I've got to find Ali and plead with him to help me. I sigh. What a dumb plan. But it's the only one I've got. Closing the diner door softly behind me, I step out on to the street and head for home.

And Stella says there are six ribbons of prayer for the Crow People but there are seven sacred directions. South, West, North, East, Sky, Earth and the Within. The seventh direction has no colour. It is hidden in the heart where it is hardest to see. But I'm looking hard, you better believe me – I'm searching high and low. I ain't gonna be a victim no more.

The sun is rising above the rooftops by the time I turn into my street, dipping the chimneys and aerials on the south side of the road in brilliant gold. As I walk the last few paces, suddenly I am caught, full in the glare, and for a few seconds I'm almost blinded. And then I stop dead, amazed. For who is directly in front of me, sitting on my top doorstep, but Ali? My hand flies up to my face to shade my eyes. Yes, it's him all right; his legs crossed at the ankle as he basks in the glow of the early morning sun.

Tilting his head, he smiles. 'Dirty stop-out. Where you been?'

'Around.'

He jerks his thumb over his shoulder. 'Want to get

some bagels? Kaiser's be open by now I reckon.'

I stare at him a long moment, heart thudding. I've just spent the whole journey home working out how to get him onboard and now here he is.

'Hello. Earth to geek boy.'

I pull myself together with an effort. 'Yeah. Just din't think I'd see you again so soon after last night . . .'

And then Ali does something strange. He bends over and, reaching for his shoelace, he suddenly starts to talk, really *talk*, like I haven't heard him talk for years.

'Listen, Anthony. I need to talk to you.' And before I have a chance to answer him, he plunges on. 'I've grown up on road and my boys, we roll like brothers, cuz that is what we are, a family, ai'ght? I know you don't get it but I had to join the Betta to *survive*. But they ain't my family, not for real, closest thing I got to that is you.'

I stare down at him, but he keeps his eyes firmly on his sneakers.'My man across the way's pushing a Mercedes. An S2000 and I'll be in one soon enough if I keep doin' good.' A brief smile flashes across his face. '*Well* before you, you loser.'

I grin. 'That's for sure.'

'So, every night I'm out earning serious P's, right? And that's what I want to tell you . . . If anything, y'know, gets messed up, I want you to know where my stash is . . . and

I want you to have it, to *keep* it, yeah? Use it for college or for Stella. Something decent, ai'ght?'

I take a step towards him, but he raises his hand to ward me off.

'There's no good saying nothing, Anthony. It's just the way it is. When I used to get hit and my dad beating on my mom and her going through madness it's kind of messed with my head.' He rubs his sneaker with his forefinger. 'So you'll take it? My money, if anything happens . . . if I tell you where it is?'

I shake my head. 'But what's going to happen to you?'

His voice drops. 'That Mustang you saw last night. That's Kit's ride.'

'The woman in the passenger seat?'

'Ai'ght.'

'Do you know her?'

'By reputation. She's a face.'

'What's she doing round here then?'

Ali shrugs. 'Don't know. The word is she's an enforcer for a senior guy.'

'Why are you telling me this now?'

Ali looks me dead in the eye. 'Is it true, that you *know* it's a Betta ordered Tais dead?'

'Yes.'

'For definite?'

175

'He's called César Desai. We've traced him as far as Bermuda.'

Ali breathes out, long and slow. 'Bermuda . . . That's us for sure, but I ain't never heard of him. But that's normal, I mean, no one ever uses their right name once they make high rank.'

'Will you help me then?'

'What's your plan?'

'I have a contact, this guy called the Teller . . .'

'Who's he?'

'I don't know. Maybe a financier, a journalist . . . a hacker? It's impossible to tell to be honest. Anyway, he knew Tais, y'know, inside the Drop . . . and day before yesterday he contacted me, offering to help find who did this to her.'

'What help has he got for you?'

'An Altform hacker ID strong enough to get us close to the Betta, to pose as a replacement for Tais.'

'Yeah, but Anthony, even if you've got a good Altform, you'd never get nowhere without an introduction.'

'I know . . .'

Ali's face tightens. 'I see. You want me to act as fixer?'

'Yes.'

'You don't want much do you? You know what they'd do to me if they knew I was crossing them?'

'You won't get caught, tho'. Not if we do it right. You'll just do the intro and they'll never link you to us.'

Ali yanks at his sneaker laces.

I scan his face. 'No?'

He furrows his brow. 'Who you're looking for will be senior. A major at least and they ain't easy to locate. I've been full in for a year and I ain't never ever seen hide nor hair of no high faces. They keep themselves well apart from us street traders.'

'What about this Kit woman? Could you reach her?'

'Maybe. But even if I could, what then?'

'A wire, see if we can get her to take us higher. Record as much as we can.'

'And then what?'

'Take it to Garcia.'

Ali turns and spits. 'Ah, Anthony – this ain't a virt. Even where the feds ain't been bought off they've been cut to the bone.'

'You think I don't know that? If there was any other way I'd do it. But this Garcia guy is still working the case. It's him or no one, Ali.'

Ali rubs his chin. 'And you want me to go to Kit because the Mustang was there at the time of Tais' hit?'

'It's the only lead we've got. We know César Desai exists, that it could be him that ordered the hit, but unless we can link him to the hit, we ain't got anything.'

Ali frowns. 'And in this fool plan of yours who am I takin' in?'

'Me.'

A gasp, and then Ali throws his head back and roars with laughter. 'Ah, Anthony, all them brains for nothin', man.'

I shrug. 'Who else is there? I know I'm no good, but I'll be in Altform, and if we can get beyond Kit to a proper meeting, I only need to be in for a few minutes to identify him. I know his voice, remember?'

'Yeah, but then it'll be just your word against his. If you're gonna record evidence for the feds, you'll need to spend time in there.'

'There's no one else I can trust.'

Our eyes meet.

'Yes there is.'

I shake my head. 'I won't ask her. It's too much.'

'Quit bein' the big hero. It's up to her, not you.'

'She told me last night she can't do any more. And she's right.'

Ali dusts his hands on his suit trousers. 'Then I'll ask her. She can't say no to me, ai'ght?'

'So you're going to help me, then?'

Suddenly Ali levers himself upright and grabs me by

the shoulder. And the boy looking into my face is the old Ali, the crazy boy who hated bullies, the one who looked out for me all those years ago.

'Yeah, but only if you promise me.'

'What?'

'That you take my stash, if things go bad for me in there?' He shakes his head. 'It killed me lettin' you go alone last night. Worse than anything the Betta could do to me.' Suddenly Ali's mouth twists in a strange smile. 'The thing is I don't even care 'bout the money. Never did. Best times for me wuz back in the day on your grandad's sofa with the D channel. *Egyptians. What were the mummies smoking in the tomb?* Cracks me up, man.'

Standing on the walkway outside Lola's apartment I hastily check the time. Eight a.m. It's pretty early to be banging on her door, but I can't lose any momentum, not now Ali is with me. Twisting my head, I check that all of him is hidden behind a pillar and then I step up to Lola's front door and flip the buzzer. In a few moments Mrs Rossi appears, holding her tiny dog in her arms. Her eyebrows lift when she sees me.

'Bit of a primitive time for social calls, isn't it, Anthony?'

I smile. 'Never too early for you, Mrs R.'

She frowns. 'Hmm. You two had a fight or something? She is in one mean mood this morning.'

'No, we're cool . . .'

Mrs Rossi steps outside. 'Well, don't just stand there like a wet hen. I'm just on my way out to walk this one.' She casts a glance upstairs. 'Go on up, but don't say I didn't warn you if you get scratched.'

I stand for a moment at the doorway, listening to the click clack of Mrs Rossi's heels as they grow fainter on the walkway. And then, sticking my fingers in my mouth, I whistle for Ali. In seconds he's by my side, looking a few shades paler than usual, if truth be told.

We step inside and I jerk my thumb towards the stairs. 'Ready?'

'Yeah.'

Reaching the landing, I pause outside Lola's bedroom and rap softly on the door. 'Lola?'

No answer, so I knock again. No answer again. Exchanging a quick glance with Ali, I gently push her door open.

'Lola?'

It takes me a couple of moments to adjust to the gloom. And then I see her, sitting in front of an angled mirror at her bedside table, brushing her hair. She turns as I enter the room, her jaw dropping in surprise. And then she freezes, says something in Spanish, something *bad* by the sound of it.

She seems to get to Ali, somehow, before he's even in the room. One minute he's standing behind me, and the next he's on his knees, gasping for breath.

I whirl around. 'Ali?'

And then I quickly turn away, trying to wipe the smile off my face as my friend clutches his stomach, weaving a strange pattern in the air with his outstretched hands.

Lola stands over him, fists bunched.

'What are you doing here?'

He sucks at the air, desperate for breath. 'You . . . kicked me.'

'I was aiming lower. I told you I never want to see you again. Ever.'

But Lola's words are drowned out as Ali doubles up in a great coughing fit.

After a minute, she rolls her eyes. 'Oh, *c'mon*. Breathe in. Count. One, two, three, four.'

After another humungous, jerking cough, Ali *finally* straightens.

Lola jerks her thumb towards the door.

'Good. Now go.'

He holds out his hand. 'Wait. Just hear me out.'

'No.'

'You have to listen to me . . . This boy will die if he goes it alone.'

Lola stares at him, her face an unreadable mask.

Ali pulls himself to his knees. 'Now I know how you feel 'bout me, but this ain't about us, this is *business*.'

Her lips form a thin line. 'Business?'

'Yeah. *Tais* business.'

I watch her face closely, see her eyes spark. He's a clever one, my friend Ali. He knows how to push Lola's buttons all right.

But she shakes her head. 'I can't believe a Betta is trying to lecture me.'

'I ain't lecturing you. It's the truth, Lola. We're never gonna escape this place if we leave her to rot with no payback. We'd be the same as them.'

'Them? *You*, you mean.'

Ali's gaze drops to the floor.

Lola flings her arms out. 'And what's the plan? Did Anthony tell you about Bermuda? You expect me to take on the Betta all by myself? I mean, *get real*.'

'You won't be alone. I'm coming too.'

A sharp breath. 'But you're *initiated*. They'll kill you for sure.'

Ali touches the jagged scar on his lower lip. 'I want in.'

Lola glares at him, a long unblinking stare. Then she looks at me.

'I hate you both.'

I gulp, fast. 'Just hear the full plan. We've got help now, from the Teller.'

'All right, Anthony. Tell me.' Lola holds up a warning forefinger. 'But don't think I'm saying yes. I'm just listening. And *if* – and it is a really big if – I decide to come in, you're not working the Drop with us.'

I jut out my jaw. 'Yes I am.'

'No you're not,' Ali and Lola both say in unison.

My fingers bunch into a fist. 'I'm not going to let you risk your lives while I sit around doing nothing.'

'But you'll get us all killed if you come in. You want that?'

'You can't stop me.'

Lola's voice softens. 'And 'sides, if we're going in we need someone external to pull it together. There's going to be a lot of locations and personnel to link up. Honest.'

We stare at each other.

'Anthony, I'm not joking. That's the deal.'

I mentally cross my fingers. 'Fine.'

'Don't think I don't know you're not crossing your fingers somewhere. I *mean* it.'

I told you she's sharp. Hydrochloric acid ain't got nothing on Lola Rossi.

'OK.'

Lola lowers herself on to the edge of her dressing table.

'So, tell me what you've got.'

'The Teller offered me an Altform hacker ID to pose as a replacement for Tais. The plan is to try and get as close as we can to César, record what we hear . . . take it to the feds.'

'What's in the ID?'

I shrug. 'Not completely sure, but from what we know about the Teller he don't do shoddy work.'

She bites her lip. 'You've got the Altform here?'

'On my deck.'

'Then I need to take a real close look.' She turns to Ali. 'What's your part?'

'Fixing up an intro.'

She nods. 'How long will you need?'

'Dunno. I'll have to make some calls to get to Kit.'

'Who's Kit?'

'She's an enforcer for a senior guy. I reckon she might be hooked somehow to Desai, but right now there ain't no way of telling. We might get lucky – maybe she reports direct to him. Or maybe there's more levels above her 'fore we can get to him, which means things ain't gonna be so easy.'

'How hard d'you think it'll be to set up a meet?'

Ali shrugs. 'My profile is good, but she's still gonna want to check me out 'fore she'll accept any kind of hook-up with an outsider.'

Lola frowns. 'How high up do you think we can really go with this? No one really important is gonna meet with an Altform hacker, right?'

'Don't know till we try. Even at high level Betta operate more face to face than you think. They like to know who your friends are, your family, before they do business with you. That way they own you for real.'

I clear my throat. 'What about me?'

Lola turns. 'You, my friend, are going to learn some link-up tricks. If we're going to pull this off, we need someone to monitor comms between us and the Associates.'

'Thought you weren't dragging them into this.'

'Yeah, but we're going to *need* at least two Associates working it, plus Ali and me – and it'll be down to you to link us all up together, to keep the communication flowing . . . and to pull us out, fast, you know, if it all goes tits up.' Lola stands, reaching for the top shelf of her bookcase. 'Here, take this simulator chip and lock yourself in your room till you've mastered it.'

Lola drops the chip into my hand, and as I fold it into my palm a rush of adrenaline streaks through my gut. Ali catches the rush too and he bursts into a grin, eyes shining.

Lola tuts. 'I didn't say yes yet.' She rubs at her arm. 'Can't believe I'm even considering this. I begged her not to go too deep.'

Ali runs his hand through his hair. 'Yeah, but people make mistakes.'

'And leave other people to pay for them.'

'Harsh. You think Tais wanted this?'

'I don't know. And I can't ask her now.' Tears spring to Lola's eyes. Ali moves towards her but she waves him away. 'Don't think this means I hate you any less.'

He freezes. 'Ai'ght. We do this for Tais, nothin' more nothin' less. And when we done, we go our separate ways. Deal?'

'I told you, I haven't said yes yet.'

'But you will.'

'Don't think you know me so well, Ali.'

Their eyes lock for a long moment. In the strained silence that follows I glance from one to the other. Ah man. Love is cruel. Love is old. Love is super old, old chemicals – oxytocin and vasopressin – rolling around in our blood. Frog chemicals. And we get addicted, y'know, to the compounds, to the way they make us feel. Literally, chemically addicted to other people. And so we're standing in Lola's room up on the twenty-second floor and it's now . . . but our genes and our chemicals and our brains don't know nothing about *now*. They are way back in the day. We're just a bunch of monkeys trying to survive. That's all we are.

Gripping the simulator chip tight in my fist, I duck out of Lola's apartment block and set off for home. And as I move along the backstreets, I've only got one thought – *I won't let her down again* – and the thought makes my blood flush to my face.

'Anthony!'

I pull up, turning towards the direction of the shout. Who's that? And then I spy him. Grandad. He's waving at me from outside a kind of shabby community centre. What's he doing here? Ah yeah, it's Saturday, his day with the Olders. Damn! I haven't got time to talk to him now, but he's patting the bench next to him. I've got to go over, I've got to give the old boy a few minutes, haven't I?

I trot over to his side and Grandad smiles up at me. 'Where are you running to?'

'Oh . . . home.'

He sighs. 'Good, good. You know, lad . . . I think I've got it all backwards, somehow. When I were your age I'd wake up and I'd think *fishing*. And I'd creep out of my bed, before anyone was up and run, *run* through the dew down to the canal. Just like you're running now.' He stretches out his legs.

'And then I grew up and had so many thoughts about things I should be doing that I stopped doing any of 'em. What a waste. I ran everywhere, y'know? Never walked. Bah! Walking was for old folk.'

I glance over his shoulder into the community centre. From here I can see a couple of old people already being parked in front of the tube for the day.

Grandad taps me on the knee. 'Bit early for you en't it tho'?'

'I – I couldn't sleep.'

He waggles his head. 'You know I were just thinking about your friend Ali. You ever see him any more?'

'Sometimes. He's living on the Estate now.'

Grandad's expression clouds. 'He's not gone over to the Betta has he?'

I shrug.

Grandad shakes his head. 'What a waste. You know, one time I had a pal, John Francis. That Ali reminded me of him. Went in the army, he did. We was at school together, ooh he was a sharp one, straight A student, never a day's trouble in his life, lovely fella. And then one night he were back home on leave and he were walking back to his ma's place and he found the body of a murdered woman in an alley just behind the Estate, the same one Ali's living on now. It were in all the papers, a bad do.'

Grandad sighs. 'And after that John just went off the rails, but I knew him, see, before it all happened. He weren't a bad man – no, Anthony, he were just in shock I s'pose, even after all that time.'

For a moment I lean my weight against the rough wood of the bench. Somebody's opened the centre window and I can hear the old folks doing their tube-lounge morning banter, to cover the shame of being forklifted in by the carers, like crates of bananas. *How you doing? Pretty good. You? Oh, mustn't grumble.*

I frown, wondering how it'll be when I'm old. Maybe we'll all have ditched our decaying bodies by then and we'll be in like a virtual old folk portal . . . with our brains plugged in, bodies in jello.

We'll be like, *Hey there* a, *hi* b, *hi* c – *long time no see!*

Look everybody – c's back! Check it out, s/he's on new medication! S/he's flying. LOL. Way2Go cccccccccccc! God I hope I get my grandad's genes and not my dad's. The thought makes me want to puke.

'Anthony?'

I turn away from the window.

'Yeah, I'm sorry, but I've got to get moving, Grandad.'

He stretches his arms out. 'What's the hurry?'

I want to tell him. I want to so much. I wish with all my heart I was still young and he could take care of things like he used to.

I mean, what do we think we're doing? Three kids taking on the Betta . . . We must be insane, right? But that's just how it is now. The feds they don't know what to do. Parents they don't know what to do. Teachers they don't know what to do. *Nobody* knows.

'*Really*. There's someone waiting on me at home.'

I bend down to hug him goodbye and suddenly Grandad does a weird thing. He leans forward and grabs me, crushing me to his chest. And then he doesn't let go, he holds me there, his arms trembling.

I don't know what to do; he's never done anything like this before. I can't breathe. I try to pull back, but he grabs me even tighter and he's crushing me so hard I can hear his old heart pounding in his bird-bone ribcage.

191

I try to pull away again and this time he releases me, and I sort of fall into the road.

Staggering backwards, it takes me a few paces to right myself and then I turn to look back at Grandad. He's staring at me, like he knows what I'm going through, but he understands it's something I've got to deal with myself. To be a man, *y'know*?

For a second I stand, rooted to the spot. And then I turn, walking away *fast* down the road. And I don't look back, not even once. No matter how much I want to.

Ali and Grandad and Stella and Tais. They've made me who I am, a person who's pretty different, unique. I'm not just *Ai'ght mate, ai'ght?* I know what it's like not to be on the winning side. I really do, y'know. And, as I approach the corner of the High Street, I break into a run once again. I'm making up for lost time, you'd better believe I am.

And now it's four hours later and I'm so mad I want to kill someone. I've just messed up a Drop-level jump for basically the thirty-thousandth time in a row.

Smacking my forehead in frustration I toss my deck on to my knees and blow out my cheeks. I must keep calm, I've not got the luxury of a meltdown. And so, snatching up the device again, I force my fingers to move more deliberately, but still with *flow*.

From watching Tais all these years, I know the Drop is all about intuition and flexibility – about seeing the possibilities and executing the right move. And from what I've observed, the less you *think*, the better you progress. It's all about *feel*. Maybe that's why I never got good at it, me being such a geek an' all.

I've got to master this jump. Gazing around my current Drop location, I reposition myself again and narrow my eyes, working out my next move through the rich tapestry of spread betting, gambling boxes and risk-roller booths lined up in front of me.

I execute a tiny point-three-degree turn and immediately the landscape warps into another zone. Now I'm smack in the middle of an open outcry pit with guys in brightly coloured jackets bellowing numbers at each other. Next to me a sweaty-faced guy lifts his hand to signal to a trader and catches me in the face with his elbow. I duck sideways, cursing. This place is way too tacky. If I'm going to be any help to Ali and Lola I've got to make the jump to a much, much deeper level.

I try to clear my mind, concentrating all my energy on the program and suddenly, I start to gain momentum.

Rolling sideways past a bank of booths, I slide between the moving lines of bending code. I'm accelerating now. Forcing my fingers to keep moving, I scan each fast-approaching junction, street and corridor and pick my path with care. I've finally cleared my mind of junk! I'm working on feel . . . and the Drop is *really* speeding up now; liquid lines of glass and metal coalescing around my body as I hurtle forward.

This is how it's meant to be – and as I grow in confidence, I can feel my muscles relaxing. This is the time to jump, now!

I punch in a code sequence. For a second it's like the whole world has slowed to nothing – a bubble of motionless, weightless corporate space – and then, with a violent jolt, I'm propelled into the middle of an energy flux, the surrounding zone dissolving into a swirling vortex directly in front of me. I grit my teeth, step towards the centre – and suddenly I'm through – I'm out the other side – and I'm standing on the sidewalk, gazing up at the Greek pillars of the New York Stock Exchange, 11 Wall Street.

I punch the air. I've done it! I've executed my first high-level solo Drop.

For a long moment I stare up at the stone exterior. It's massive. But what's blowing my mind ain't the size of the place, it's that the building is so raggedy looking. A trickle of traders straggles past me on the marble steps, but apart from that the place looks half closed.

I've heard about the collapse of the Exchange, of course. But it's one thing to hear about a thing; it's another to see it, even if it's only from inside the Drop.

I remember the day of the crash – I came home from school, turned on the tube and right there, in that moment, I knew things were never going to be the same again. Onscreen was a graph thing with a red line plunging downward off the monitor. Seven hundred points lost in a day, twenty per cent of the Exchange's total value, and the same thing happening for the next three days.

And the thing I remember most at the time was everyone kept saying it was going to be OK. All week I flipped through the tube channels, looking for someone who wasn't clinically insane to say something true, but all I got was news anchors and economists and politicians screaming and gibbering and promising it was all going to be OK, even as we swirled down the plughole. I don't blame them or nothing; they were only trying to keep us calm with *words*. Humanity's big weapon. Not bullets or knives or gunpowder or nukes. *Just words*. Tiny little sounds to keep us from going mad with fear

in the dark night and what a bunch of bozos we are
& what's the big deal about language anyway¿¿
in reality_loads of other animals_have_it +++ theres
these_little punky desert rats intexas with a ^whole
l a n g u a g e _ _ v e r b s + n o u n s
+adjectives – the lot)) andtheysay things
like *that-coyote-there-he's-the one*
who pretends to*walk past but@
the=last minute he jumps for_you!
**watch him!

it/s-not-just-us-who's-got-language+++we're not so
special you know.....parrots*whales*wolves*dolphins
they got language too= and_do_youknowthe/// +creature
s+who've+got+the+best+language+on+earth??

IT"Sthehunted ones**the superhunted
the^ones-who+live::for=a=longtime,

in ^tight+social=groups. Its-
them_because   they_are))the((most scared
creatures+and yeah ++ didyouknow
americansrelease_fiftymillionkilos_
ofcrap**every+singleday??
. . . 1.8millionkilosanhourseventeenbillionkilos
ayear ¿

Lets>>talk)about/that)))right?

and all I'm saying*is
maybe sometimes we
should be scared++
And we should use
that fear to face up to
what we're doing to
the world and stop
doing it***))

Suddenly the cool plastic of my deck pulses in my hand. Tearing my eyes from the Stock Exchange pillars, I look down at my screen.

LOLA108: Teller Altform ID is genius.

I smile. *AGRIFFIN: Does that mean you're in?*

LOLA108: Yeah. But fast, Anthony. Drop and record. No hero shit.

AGRIFFIN: Agreed.

LOLA108: Now get your ass out of Wall Street and start working the link-up.

AGRIFFIN: How d'you know where I am?

LOLA108: Puh-lease.

AGRIFFIN: Drop snob.

LOLA108: No don't take it like that. You did a good jump, my friend.

A grin spreads across my face. Compliments from LR are as rare as hens' teeth, as my grandad says.

LOLA108: I'm sending you thru Gabe and Emli's details right now. They're the Associates I trust the most. They'll do the complex ID exchange stuff, which leaves you live feed, camera/audio monitoring plus heart rate/pressure for emergency pull out. Think you can handle it? It's all on the chip if you get stuck.

AGRIFFIN: How long have I got?

LOLA108: As long as it takes Ali to fix up a meet. It's

up to him now.

Flipping my deck shut, I take one last look along Wall Street. Then, bracing myself, I make the jump back home.

It's late evening by the time we're ready. Up in my room, Lola and Ali sit facing me across the bed. Lola glances at my door. 'Your mom definitely working the night shift?'

'Won't be back till six at the earliest.'

Ali drums his fingers, restless. 'So who's on backup with Anthony?'

'Gabe in Baltimore, and Emli in Bangkok. Gabe's handling all the personnel stuff, Emli security.'

He glances at me. 'And you're cool your end?'

'Yeah. I've got comms lines set up between all four of you. Camera, audio and . . .' I tap the glowing key on my deck, 'emergency decompression.'

Ali lifts an eyebrow. 'Check the boy out. But I still don't get how you're gonna record everything we say.'

Lola snorts. 'Associates are on it. Basically every time either of us shifts inside the Drop, Anthony punches the new coordinates through to Gabe and Emli, and one of them will Altform into an employee, y'know someone who *belongs* there, so there'll always be a camera recording us. It's the only way we can be clean when the Betta scan us, which they definitely will do.'

Ali nods. 'For sure, soon as we Drop. But how will the Associates be able to tail us?'

I lean forward. 'As soon as I pass on the new data, Emli bores through the Drop company's security system, followed by Gabe seconds later. It's his job to fake up the worker's history and insert the new data into the company's systems and then pull out before anyone notices. You won't see any of this from where you are, but you can know for sure that the barman shaking up a cocktail, the driver in the car, the guy cleaning the toilets . . . will be an Associate, capturing your every word.'

Ali sighs. 'Ai'ght, sounds convincing enough. But just don't mess up your part, yeah? It's my head on the line.'

'I won't.'

He turns to Lola. 'Don't push it too far with Kit, right? This your first meet and she's gonna be sniffin' round you like a wolf in case you're a trap.'

Lola flushes. 'Watch your own back too. You're as

much of a threat to her as me. I mean, as far as she's concerned, you're a nobody, just a street-level guy who might be out to trash her.'

Ali flushes in his turn. I glance from one to the other.

'You guys going to be all right?'

'Yeah – why shouldn't we be?' Lola shoots back.

I twist my deck to face me. This is all I need – a soap opera on top of everything else.

'Time to get in position. Any time now.'

Lola starts to unlace her sneakers.

Ali reaches for his 'trodes. 'I don't see why we got to lay down.'

Lola shakes her head. 'We've been through this. We just don't know how deep we're going in this trip. It's safer this way.'

He sighs but, folding his jacket under his head for a pillow, he stretches out on the bed, Lola joining him moments later.

I lift my hand. 'What do you want to do about me pulling you out?'

Lola's eyes meet mine from behind her visor. 'It's your call. I – I trust you.'

Ali throws me a swift glance. 'Me too, you geek. But let this thing run as far as she can. I ain't never doin' this again.'

Suddenly the deck lights up.

KIT: *Now*.

A long string of coordinates scroll across the screen.

Ali blows out his cheeks. 'Ready when you are. We've got two minutes to Drop before the Betta gate goes cold.'

I lean forward, poised to push the coordinates on to Gabe.

There's a knock at the bedroom door.

Heart in mouth, I turn. 'What?'

'I need help.'

I let out a breath. Stella.

Lola waves her arm. 'Get rid of her!' she whispers.

'Help with what?' I say, trying to keep my voice calm. If I shout, she'll freak out.

'My homework.'

'I can't come right now. Can you do something else for a while?'

'Like what?'

'I don't care. Anything.'

'Like what?'

'I don't know.'

The door handle rattles.

I jump to my feet. 'Stel, don't come in!'

Lola slams her hand on the bed. 'Do something, quick!' she hisses, urgently.

Stella's voice is turning into a whine. 'Why can't I?'

I glance at the time. Only one minute twenty seconds left. Crossing the room in one bound, I open the door and squeeze outside. Stella is standing in the hallway with muddy boots on.

'Where you been?'

'Crow park.'

I bite back my irritation. 'Look, I'm busy right now.'

She looks past me into the room.

'Why are Ali and Lola here?'

I move my body to block her. '*Stella*. I promise I'll come out as soon as I can. I ain't doing this to be hard on you.'

She tugs viciously on her right boot, yanking it off her foot. 'You're stupid.'

I spread my hands. 'Go and work on your journal, yeah?'

Stella turns on her heel, raising her voice for the benefit of Lola and Ali.

'I don't want to come in anyway. Losers!'

For a second I watch her thudding down the hallway – sock, boot, sock, boot – and then I turn and race back into the room. Diving to my knees, I attach the 'trodes to my temples and put my visor on. Twenty-five seconds left.

'Ready?'

'Yes!' cries Ali. 'Now!'

I punch in Kit's coordinates and, for a moment, the room blurs and spins as I am sucked to the edge of the Drop. And then I pull back into reality, just as Lola and Ali's bodies go limp on the bed, their eyes falling back in their sockets as their minds enter the program. And then a wave of panic splashes acid up through my belly, my chest. I stare at them, wide-eyed. There's no turning back now.

Wrenching my gaze from them, I turn to my deck screen, waiting, *one, two, three* seconds before the video feed springs to life. And when it appears, it's hard at first to work out what's going on – I catch a quick glimpse of ornate ironwork arches and then suddenly the screen pans to the left, and then back to the right again. I frown, trying to get a fix on the visual. Why is the shot moving like this? And then I figure it out as I catch sight of Gabe reflected in a window. Dressed in dirty green overalls, he moves along a passageway between market-stall booths, sweeping the floor with slow, deliberate strokes.

I breathe a sigh of relief. The Associates are on point. It's taken them only seconds to generate Gabe's fake reference, work permit and payroll history before slotting his Altform in as a legit worker in the Drop.

Now the camera pans along the stalls – it looks like they're in an antiques arcade – until I finally catch sight of Ali and Lola. They've paused to browse in a jewellery shop window. I suck in a breath. Lola is over two metres tall in her heels, a shimmering green cocktail dress sweeping from her shoulders all the way to the floor. She towers over Ali, who fidgets by her side in a cheap, shiny suit, too short in the arms and the legs. I stifle a laugh. Lola's dressed him up like a waiter. She's never going to give the guy a break, even in Altform.

Lola bends to look closely at a shelf of Swarovski crystal animals, while Ali jerks his cuffs down so they cover his wrists, and for a moment, I turn from the screen and gaze at their bodies lying side by side on my bed. Insanity.

And then the camera pans back along the arcade aisles again. The girl who walks towards them is slight, her light, coffee-coloured skin taut on her bones. She's impossible to age – anything from eight to thirteen years old. This has to be Kit, in Altform, because flanking her are two Betta guards. I tilt my deck, zooming in on their long, powder-blue, kid-leather jackets. Both are packing revolvers. The one on the right is carrying a row of stun grenades strapped to his belt.

Ali turns, meets Kit's eye. The girl indicates for both him and Lola to raise their arms. Submitting to a full body frisk from one of the bodyguards, they are scanned electronically by the second man, who closely monitors his reader before signalling the all clear. Kit then strides into the antiques shop and sits down on a chaise longue at the rear of the premises, the guards taking up their positions alongside her. Ali and Lola follow her inside. So far so good.

Kit points towards a chair. 'Please, sit.'

Lola sinks down on to a low chair opposite her.

'Your name is Anna Cortez?'

Lola nods.

'You've also worked under Lisa Mendez, Adi Opoku, Tomoko Shimizu.'

'Yes, I've worked under those IDs.'

'Independently?'

'Yes.'

Kit watches Lola, her blue eyes expressionless. 'And now you say you wish to work for us?'

'Yes.'

'Why now? Surely you must've been making money?'

Lola shakes her head. 'Not enough. It's all scraps when you work legitimate. But in a month I've got to hand over my tuition fees . . . I need cash, fast.'

Kit glances at Ali. 'What is your history on her?'

He shrugs. 'IQ 142. Speaks fluent Spanish, Portuguese, Russian. Eighteen months working deep. She's ready for the Quantum Level.'

'You could say the same for a dozen Debtbelter kids in this city. Why her?'

'She's special.'

Kit leans back against the leather sofa and crosses her arms. 'How so?'

'She's got *flow*. Like I ain't seen since Tais.'

Kit's eyes flash. 'Don't you dare mention names in here. What are you, some kind of idiot?' The bodyguard on her right tenses, but after a moment she relaxes her shoulders and his hands move away from his holster.

Kit slides a polka-dot pink satchel from her shoulder.

'Where have you been tonight, Ali?'

'The Estate, couple of pick-ups.'

I glance at Ali's heart monitor. Rising to 120BPM.

'Keep cool, Ali,' I mouth.

'You've just made captain, yes?'

'Yes.'

'Well, the word on the street is you are a comer, but I also know for a fact that you have a personal connect with this girl. Why didn't you tell me this before?'

'No need.'

'Why not?'

Ali leans forward. 'Let's just say, the more I know someone the more likely they are to stay true. On my word, Kit, this trade is good.'

Kit's eyes meet his. 'Pretty sure of yourself, right?'

'I'm just telling you how it is. My old life is done. This girl knows it.'

Kit looks from Ali to Lola.

'Maybe so. I'm going to need to see her in action for myself.'

Lola cuts in. 'Likewise.'

Kit sucks in a breath. 'What's that supposed to mean?'

'I want to see how you operate before I work for you.'

'The Betta don't offer previews.'

Lola starts to rise. 'Then I guess I don't work for you.'

Kit holds up a hand. 'But our word is always good. Finish the job, stay alive and we will pay you. *Well.* That's our deal.' She gazes across at Lola's elegant figure. 'You think you can stay alive?'

'Yes.'

Kit smiles. 'Let's see, shall we?'

Lola's lips part in surprise. 'Now?'

'Why not? You only get one chance with the Betta. So let's find out if you're as good as Ali says you are.'

I watch as Lola's adrenaline levels rise, but in the antiques store her voice remains as calm as ever.

'Fine.'

Kit reaches inside her bag, pulls out a slip of paper. 'Here are the numbers. You've got sixty seconds.' She touches the guards' arms lightly. 'And Drop lines for all of us.'

My finger moves over to the decompression key. It's time to pull them out.

And then a message appears onscreen.

LOLA108: *First class tickets. Drop Hong Kong. ID flight attendant. Now.*

I hesitate. It's obvious what Lola wants to do, but it's too dangerous. Who knows what Kit has got in mind? My finger hovers over the button. But on the other hand, this might be our only chance to push through to the next level. We might never get back here again. Slowly I move my finger away from the decompression key and punch the new coordinates through to the Associates. I'll give it another few minutes.

Immediately my deck comes to life as Emli's commands begin to execute. In the left hand corner a window opens: a drill bit boring a wormhole through the Drop China Air firewall – followed by a sub-command generating five tickets for Hong Kong, flight 2043. And then Gabe's feed comes to life on the right hand side of the screen and I watch in amazement as the HR payroll protocol for flight attendant Gabe McQueen is created, dated and stored in superfast succession.

The windows close and as soon as the wormhole slides shut it's my turn to pull up some info. Tapping in a search, I call up a cabin plan and, scanning the interior carefully, find a suitable recording position for Gabe. With only ten seconds left on the clock I transmit all the data through to Lola.

My deck screen darkens again and I wait in horrible silence, willing the video feed to hook up. After a long moment of brain chilling static, finally it does, the screen brightening into the interior of the China Air first class cabin. I let out a stream of breath between my teeth. We're on our way.

In the cabin, Lola and Kit sit side by side, Ali and the bodyguards a few rows behind. From the right hand windows I catch a glimpse of the brilliant lights of Drop Hong Kong coming into view below. I frown. Somehow I must have lost a whole chunk of time in the Drop transfer. Suddenly Lola comes into sharp view as Gabe moves towards her in the cabin.

She turns to Kit. 'How long do I have?'

'One hour.'

'And you won't tell me anything more about my mission?'

Kit purses her lips. 'No. It's down to you to figure it out.'

Lola glances down at the city unfolding below. 'You won't even tell me who I'm working for?'

The girl cocks her head to one side. 'If you're good enough you'll find out. You've already passed the flight test, so let's see what else you can do.'

Three rows back, Ali shifts, restless in his seat.

The engine sound alters as the plane begins its descent. All of a sudden my screen blurs as the plane falls through a pocket of air – I reach forward to refocus – but before I can adjust the input, the cabin tips wildly, slamming the passengers back in their seats. Straining to see, all I can make out is Lola's terrified face before my deck cuts out.

I stare at the blank screen in panic. The screen is totally dead – all comms are down, including Gabe and Emli's feed. I've got no way to pull Lola and Ali out! And then, as fast as it disappeared, the screen flickers back to life.

The controls are still greyed out, but at least I've got a visual. I peer desperately at the grainy, low-qual feed. What am I seeing? I can just about make out a crowd; people slipping through the darkness as the camera lurches from left to right. Then I see torches flaring up and what looks like a series of lanterns slide by, as the camera operator climbs a set of steps before turning into a dark alleyway.

I force myself to *think*. If I panic I'll lose them for real. I'm going to have to take this one stage at a time. Ali.

Check him first. I've got no visual at *all* for him, the only reading I've got is his heartbeat, pulsing a steady feed. Well, at least he's alive. Quickly I shift across to Lola's feed. Again, her heart rate is strong and steady, but like Ali she's totally vanished. I guess Gabe must be there recording for me to be seeing this, but I've totally lost my connect with him too. Some link-up man I am.

There's just no way I can tell if this is a simple disrupt or if it's the Betta blocking my feed, but for sure this ain't right. I can't let it go on like this. It's time to pull them out. Slamming my thumb down on the decompression key, I pray it's still working. I turn to stare at Ali and Lola, their bodies motionless on the bed. A second flicks by, and then another. Neither of them move. I hit the key again. *Still no movement.*

I ball my hands into fists, pressing my nails deep into the flesh. This can't be happening . . . Keep focused, Anthony. Keep with them. My only option right now is the flickering visual feed on my screen. I've got no choice but to follow it and hope that the link reconnects.

Onscreen, the input visual suddenly flares into dazzling light as Gabe turns into a brightly lit market street; a brash thoroughfare packed with busy shoppers. I stare at their faces. It looks like we're on the ground in Hong Kong, but where exactly? We pass a man as he lifts noodles from a wide metal pan, steam gushing up into the night air, and then the camera pans to the left and I catch a glimpse of stacked wooden trays, loaded with oysters, seahorses, starfish. Weird shit.

And then there's a sudden jerk in the opposite direction. Now I'm looking at stalls selling old ornaments – vases, jars, knickknacks – and suddenly the viewer pauses in front of a smeared antique mirror and I catch a flash of red hair, a swirl of green dress from across the aisle. It's Lola! Fumbling for the decompression button, I bang my fist down on the key, but just as I hit it, my visual connection flickers and dies again. Too late!

Heart racing, I turn again to stare at my two lifeless friends on the bed. I want so badly to reach out, to wake them. My deck dials turn from orange to red . . . Lola's levels are peaking up into the red zones, her neurotransmitters pumping out endorphins. She must be in bad pain. I throw the deck to the floor and reach out to touch her shoulder, desperate to shake her awake. It takes all my strength of will to pull my hand back, but I manage it. It'd be suicide to pull her out from so deep. She'd die from those bends, believe me.

I grab the deck again, trying a thousand different routes to contact Gabe and Emli, but no matter what I do the device remains static; a black empty box in my hands.

The room starts to swim around me as I feel the first waves of deep panic – and then *finally* my deck comes back to life. Bringing it up to my face I can just see Lola. She's lying in some dark space and it looks like it's raining, in heavy tropical sheets.

'Come on Lola, get up!' I scream.

Slowly she moves and, rolling to her knees, she brushes her wet hair out of her eyes. Behind her is a dark, blue-black void. What's that? The sea? Abruptly, the camera pulls back a few paces and for a moment I'm able to observe the whole scene – a crowded waterfront, with stalls and merchants everywhere and a rotten pier running into the sea.

And then there's another burst of dazzling light, followed by a great roar that rises from the surrounding area. Lola looks up, her eyes widening in fear. The camera pulls back again and now I can see what she sees – a huge crowd, seated high above her on bleachers that climb into the air in a semi-circle of sharply sloping concrete tiers. I narrow my eyes, trying to make sense of what I'm seeing. What is this place? The arena looks like it's just been dumped on top of the waterfront, like the Betta have mashed two levels together for their own purposes. This must be the Quantum Level.

The camera pans around the crowd, their faces a joined

web of fierce excitement as they start to chant for Lola to rise to her feet. Great plumes of smoke billow from street level, creating a mist-like aura around the stage as the lights play over the metal struts that support the gallery.

And then from the rear of the arena come Kit's two Betta guards. No sign of Kit herself, though. Stripped of their long blue jackets, the boys walk tall and clean, with a street fighter's gait. The taller of the two walks up to Lola, a ragged, rusting Mohican spearing out from his shaved head.

'You mind if I check you're clean for the crowd?'

He raises his hands to Lola's neck, his fingers brushing her collarbone.

'This is a legitimate show.' He winks at the crowd. 'And it's my duty to keep it that way, ai'ght?'

The crowd roars with laughter.

'Get your hands off me!' Lola twists violently, kicking out at him, but the guard pushes her backwards while the other comes up and grabs her legs, throwing her to the ground. Lola screams, thrashing her body from side to side. Suddenly the guard's hands tighten on her throat, cutting off all sound except muffled chokes.

I stare at the screen in horror. Where's Ali? For sure if he helps her the Betta will know he's a traitor, but he's got no choice now, right? And what's going on with Gabe? If this is him recording, how can he just watch Lola suffer? Maybe he can't access her.

Onstage, Lola makes another desperate effort to escape. With a violent twist, she rips free of the hands at her throat and turns, sinking her teeth into the guard's arm. He screams in agony and rolls off her body. The crowd yells. This girl's a fighter!

Blood is trickling down the first bodyguard's wrist. He signals to his partner to stay back and then rises to his feet again. Smiling, he pulls something from his sleeve. A razor. Fear slides between my shoulder blades. Is this what the Betta test is? A fight to the death?

Vomit rises to my throat. Lola is now crouched low on the concrete. The guard advances on her, sweeping the razor in front of him in a graceful, repeating arc. The crowd roars. And then he leaps at her, executing vicious cuts in the air as Lola desperately jerks backwards. And then the boy changes his grip, his arm now bent for a vicious downward stab – Lola screams in terror – and then suddenly his arm is yanked backwards, twisted violently, and he is thrown to the ground. Hope fills my mind. Is this Ali?

But I can only see where the camera lens points and it's now focusing on the right side of the stage, where the other Betta is racing forward, his hands held up in a diagonal thrust from his barrel-like chest. And then the camera pans again. It *is* Ali! The Betta bearing down on him, I watch my friend as he lurches to the right before bringing up his left foot, catching the guard in his belly. The boy staggers back, clutching his gut – and taking her chance, Lola scrabbles to her feet and plunges her stiletto heel into his throat directly beneath his jaw. The guard rolls to the floor, gasping for air, and then lies still.

By now the other guard is on his feet again. To the screams of the crowd, he comes up behind Ali, grappling him in a great bear hug, and for a few moments they are locked in the centre of the ring until Ali somehow manages to yank himself free. Smashing his knee into his opponent's chest, he hurls him forward, the momentum sending the Betta crashing into a row of stalls and scattering seafood and crushed ice across the edge of the ring and over the street. Ali waits for him rise, but the boy stays down, a trickle of blood seeping down his forehead. Ali then slowly turns to Lola and smiles, before himself lurching forward in a strange sideways stagger and slowly sinking to his knees.

The auditorium falls silent. Lola runs across the stage, reaches Ali just as he collapses on to the cold concrete. She turns him over. On his side is a red patch, spreading across his shirt. Lola tugs the fabric up to reveal a long, deep cut across his belly. The Betta must have stabbed him when they locked together. I watch in helpless horror as Ali's head falls back against the ground; as Lola rips off her jacket, wadding it up and pressing it to his torso, her lips moving as she pleads for help . . . Again and again I press the decompression key, but there is no contact and I am utterly powerless to help them.

And then suddenly Gabe's voice breaks through on my audio feed.

'Pull them out, we're flooding the Betta wall!'

'I can't! I'm locked out!' I shout.

'Yes you can. We've overridden their system. Do it now!'

My deck controls abruptly flare into life again – and slamming my finger on the decompression key, I turn to stare at Lola and Ali on the bed, praying, pleading to any God who'll listen to bring them back – and then Lola's body twitches, a hard, convulsive jerk. Choking, gasping for air she surfaces, curling herself into a tight ball on the bed. Dropping my deck I grab her by the shoulders and pull her tight to me.

'Ali!' she gasps, struggling. We turn together and my heart plummets. He isn't out!

'Decompress him!' Lola screams.

'I have.'

Grabbing my deck, Lola tries to pull him out, but nothing works. No matter what she does, Ali makes no move, no sound.

'Gabe, what's happening?' I cry.

'*We're doing everything we can, but we've lost him somehow . . .*' Gabe's voice fades out and the screen blanks again. The Betta have blocked them off.

'Oh, look.'

I turn. Lola is pointing at Ali, at the blood seeping through his shirt. Dropping the deck, she takes his hands in hers, rubs them gently.

'He's cold, Anthony.'

Suddenly the screen comes to life once more and Kit's voice comes through on the speakers.

KIT: Excellent work. Not many can break our wall. Be ready for the next level.

I punch in *re>message*, my fingers clumsy on the keys.

AGRIFFIN: What have you done to Ali?

KIT: He's ours, we deal with him as we want.

AGRIFFIN: He's hurt.

KIT: That's our business.

AGRIFFIN: He needs a doctor.

KIT: He's a big boy. At 5 a.m. you will receive new coordinates. Be ready.

AGRIFFIN: What if we don't want to continue?

221

KIT: *If you want to see Ali again you will come.*

AGRIFFIN: *He's a hostage?*

KIT: *Drop at 5 a.m. and you will understand everything. My boss wants to meet the girl.*

Lola holds out her hand.

'Pass me the deck and find something to press against the wound. There's got to be a way of getting him free.'

Seizing a towel from the back of a chair, I press it against Ali's belly while Lola tries to reroute around the Betta wall, but there's no escape, it's around us like a steel trap, completely cutting off access even to Gabe and Emli. Finally Lola hurls the deck down on to the pillows. 'I can't break through by myself. Betta are just too good.'

'Don't give up, Lola – listen, Gabe's still there on the ground, and . . . and the Associates will have gotten half the Debtbelt working on a breakthrough by now, for sure.' I'm gabbling in panic, but Lola's not even listening.

She leans over Ali. 'How's he doing?'

'Better, I think.'

I pull the towel away, and for a moment the wound is clean.

I bite my lip. 'That's it.'

Lola frowns. 'You reckon?'

But then it begins to come again, the red oozing out of

222

the cut. I slap the towel back in position and press down once more.

Lola runs her hands through her hair. 'We've got to get him to a doctor, this cut is really deep.'

I shake my head. 'How could he do anything with Ali still *inside*? 'Sides, the blood *is* much less now. We've just got to sit tight for the Associates.'

'And what if they don't break the Betta wall? Kit only gave us six hours before my next jump.'

I shake my head. 'No way you're going back in, Lola. Not on your own.'

'No choice. As soon as Kit's new coordinates come I'm in. With or without backup.'

'I said no way.'

'It isn't your decision. *I won't leave him!*'

'But there's no guarantee you'll even find him there. We can't trust them.'

'So, what's your plan? Sit here and watch another friend die in front of you?'

'No!'

'So I go in. It's the only way—'

'It's too dangerous.'

Lola swallows. 'I've already passed the first test. I'm not throwing away all our hard work for nothing. And 'sides, didn't Kit say someone wants to meet me?

223

This is our big chance . . . for *Tais*, Anthony.'

I scan Lola's face. She's a mess. Huge dark circles under her eyes, her skin a pale mask. I don't know what to say. I can't let her go back in again alone, can I?

'Let's give the Associates a few hours, see if they come up with something first.' I put my hand on her shoulder. 'But now you've got to get some rest, at least a couple hours, otherwise you'll be no good to anyone.'

I peer under Ali's towel. 'The blood's stopped, for real. He kind of looks like he's sleeping to me.'

Lola's face relaxes a little, and even as I reposition the towel on Ali's wound, she slumps back on the cushions, her eyes closing as the Drop adrenaline drains from her body. And by the time I straighten again, she's already out, her arm flung over Ali's chest.

I sit for a long, long moment, watching them breathe. And then it hits me – that *this is it*. I clench my fist. I've got to be ready because what's coming up, it ain't a test. I need to get myself ready, because like Stella says when you do something for real, you should burn *yourself* completely – like a good bonfire – and leave no trace of yourself, just *ashes*, so you can become someone new.

I think I maybe black out. One minute I'm up in my room and the next I'm down in the back yard and I've gotten a pile of my stuff stacked in front of me. I pull myself together. This ain't no time for blackouts.

Sneakers, clothes, games, I sweep as much as I can into my arms, wires and cables hanging off of me like hair, like I'm a crazy hairy homeless guy. And then I cross the yard, dumping everything against the brick wall. I don't want it any more; I don't want *anything* holding me back.

I take out a can of lighter fluid from my jacket pocket and fling a great arc of liquid over the pile. And then I stop. Suddenly I feel calm, I feel good. Bending down, I search for something to get the party started. An old shoebox lies half buried under a heap of old games. I yank the lid off and a stack of back in the day photos and postcards slide out. Bending down, I start to rake through the contents with my fingers – I pick up my dad's wedding invitation with little bells and ribbons on it – and then I drop it as I catch sight of a piece of folded newspaper. I smile. Yeah, this is the thing. Picking the paper up, I unfold it. Now *this* is ritual.

Taking out a lighter, I hold the flame to the edge. The newspaper browns, curls, and a corner of paper glows, before flickering and catching light. I toss it on to the pile and immediately green flames shoot up amongst the consoles and the air fills with the stench of burning plastic.

'Anthony?'

I turn. Stella, dressed in her pyjamas, is staring up at me.

She tugs urgently at my sleeve. 'What are you doing?'

I bend down, struggling to pull her in focus. It's like she's cut out, her face flickering in front of me.

'Look Stel, I've got something for you. It's the only thing I kept.'

I reach inside my pocket, take out a gold locket.

Stella frowns.

'Don't you want it?' I ask.

'But it's mine, anyway. It's from when I was little with my hair in it.'

Girl, 17, left for dead after 6th storey plunge from walkway

'They beat her and then pushed her over the edge'

A horrific attack involving a local girl took place yesterday, the ferocious assault apparently occuring in broad daylight at the infamous crime hotspot, known locally only as the Estate.

The as yet unnamed girl was severely beaten before being pushed from a fifth floor walkway.onto the courtyard below. .

A group of masked youths were seen fleeing the scene but as yet the police have made no arrests. Despi"

'Yeah, but you gave it to me.'

She looks from the locket to me, unsure. 'I don't get it.'

I swallow, putting on my best normal face.

'It's like how you said with the Crow Indians; it's my extension object. My possession that's all mine, that's part of me . . . for if I'm not here.'

A beat. 'Where are you going?' she asks.

'Nowhere. I didn't say I was going nowhere.'

'Anywhere. You can't go nowhere.' Stella takes a pace backwards. 'Anthony, what's going on?'

'Nothing.'

And suddenly Stella looks me right in the eye. 'You don't tell me the truth because you think I can't handle it like everybody else. You think you understand me, but you're just the same as all the others.'

'No I'm not!'

'Then stop lying to me.'

I stand there and this crazy idea of telling my sister, my little sister, fills my head. Oh God, I'd love to tell someone. But she'd freak, she'd flip. She's eleven for Christ's sake. But she's staring at me, her eyes clear and steady and suddenly it's like I can see her really clearly, like I'm seeing her for the first time.

'I've got to do something, Stel. It's the not doing anything, letting it slide, that's killing me, y'know? I don't want to live like a parasite no more . . .' I kick a pair of sneakers into the fire. 'I don't want to live like people live. *Blind. Dumb.* I don't belong nowhere – d'you know what I mean, Stel? I hate the way people's mouths move when they tell lies and they tell lies the whole time. But I don't want to be like them, I want to be alive, I want that so bad . . .' I stammer to a halt, my breath coming in hard gasps.

Stella stands there next to my melting games console, flame light glinting off her hair and she's staring up at me and she's listening, I mean, she's *really listening to me.* Suddenly my heart lifts. If somebody listens to you for real, it's something, it's something massive. It really *is, right?* And then Stella, she does the best thing. She reaches out and takes the locket from my hand and she puts it around her neck.

'Thank you. I'm glad you saved it from the fire.' She looks up. 'But you're not running away, you mean it when you say that?'

'No.'

She pokes at the now smouldering sneakers with her slipper toe. 'Because you don't have to run away, you've just got to see what's in front of you. I see new stuff all the time by getting up really early and sitting still in the garden and watching the crows.' Stella shakes her head.

'Things are interesting because you *think* about them, Anthony, not because you go somewhere different.'

I frown. 'Why are you talking like I'm dying or something?'

'I don't want you to go away.'

'I won't, *promise*. I mean, I have to for an hour, but I'll be back 'fore you know it.'

'But it's three a.m.'

'I know, but I've got no choice.'

'Where are you going?'

'The hospital.'

A small wrinkle crinkles her nose. 'But I'll see you later, right?'

'Yeah. Ali and Lola are here so you'll be safe. They're sleeping tho', so don't wake them up.'

Stella nods.

I check the fire, it's just a pile of smouldering trash now.

'One hour and I'll be back.'

'OK.'

I feel her eyes on me as I walk out of the garden. I focus on keeping my walk calm and cool. But once I turn the corner of the house and I'm out of Stella's sight, I let loose. My body feels so full of power and strength. I'm running like a devil, you'd better believe I am. I'm making up for lost time.

Gasping for air, I race along the hospital corridors, battering through the endless sets of double doors until I finally stand outside her room. Taking a deep breath, I twist the door handle and go in. Inside, it takes me a full minute before I can make myself look into her face. Oh, Tais! She twitches, strings of drool twisting round the plastic tube in her mouth, smearing her cheek. The nurses shut and open her eyes depending on whether it's day or night. Now they're closed. Oh God, she's freaking me out. She's making my flesh crawl. I stare at the plug socket, at the wires from all the machines that surround her running into it.

It's a regular socket, like the one you plug all your stuff into at home. But this electricity is plugged directly into Tais. Into her veins, where all the elements and energy in the universe are held together and the whole universe is repeated over and over and over and it's life. And it's coming from a plain old plug socket. I mean, I could just bend down and flick Tais off at the wall.

And even though I'm freaking out at the same time something is tearing apart, expanding in my mind. I swing my arms, trying not to flip out. Does she know I'm here? Does she forgive me? I try to think of something, anything I can do. *Anything*. But there's nothing. I'm helpless. And then I do the only thing that comes into my mind.

Clambering on to the bed, I grab her. I press my chest, my heart, against hers, trying to pour all my strength into her. All my strength, my life, my blood, my soul, my living energy – I try to force it into her, directly from my heart to hers, to cut through her flesh, through the chest bone, straight into her heart. I will her to live, to come back.

I remember the first time. The first time I felt her lips on mine. Oh that feeling, y'know, that she'd chosen me. That she wanted me. *Stupid me*, oh the glorious rush and the twist inside my belly! Oh, why won't she wake up? I grab her hand and I start to plead with her.

'*Come back, Tais, for me . . .*'

But she doesn't move and I lie there, clinging on to her like a drowning man. What's her side of the story? I want to shake her, I want to flick a switch and make energy shoot into all her veins. Oh man, her head is freaking me out. It's shaved on one side, her hair growing back in straggly clumps. She doesn't even look like Tais any more, but I can't go on without her. And all anyone ever knows about evolution is that survival of the fittest stuff, but what it really means is that no creature can survive by itself. *And Darwin says each creature must extract energy in order to struggle, so as to maintain its form, to live – and it must also give energy so that other forms may live.* I slam my hand down on the bed. Oh Tais, my stupid messed-up genius girl, what did I ever give you? And now you're gone I can't survive without you.

Suddenly my deck vibrates in my jacket pocket.

Sliding gently off the bed, I read the message.

LOLA108: Kit has just sent us a 2-hour warning. You need to get back here. I can't do this alone.

I snatch up Tais' hand and kiss it. Bending low over her I whisper in her ear, 'I love you.'

And there are three kinds of mammals. Prey, predator and scavenger. We think we are predators but really we are scavengers. No better'n jackals we are. But I stand there with my girl's hand tight in mine and I make a vow to be *more*. I ain't picking up the scraps this time. For once in my life I want to be the real deal – a creature with honour, with guts, with guile, with grace. A real live *human animal*.

Four forty-five a.m. Crouching by my bed, I watch as Lola gently dresses Ali's wound. A light sweat coats his forehead as he lies motionless under her hands.

'How is he?'

She shrugs. 'You're right, the bleeding has stopped – but I don't know . . . He's been under for so long, Anthony – it must be messing up his brain big time.'

'How are they holding him against his will?'

'No idea. But listen to his breathing . . . it's all shallow, like he's really struggling in there. Sooner I get inside, the better.'

I tap the deck. 'You get through to Gabe or Emli?'

Her eyes narrow. 'Nope. Betta have completely cut our connect. So I've worked out another way to communicate with you from *inside* – basically I've generated a massive bunch of minute anonymous connections across the global Debtbelt network. I figure it'll be impossible for the Betta to control that many link-ups.'

'But without Gabe you'll have no way of recording.'

'I'm going to do it myself.'

I shake my head. 'No way. You know they're going to scan you from the minute you enter the Drop.'

'They know me now . . . so there's a good chance they won't frisk me this time. Plus I'm using a micro-lens.'

'But even if they don't catch the lens, they'll pick up your video transmission signal.'

'Hopefully not. Like I was saying, I'm going to split it into a million bits. It'll be impossible to trace the feed unless someone's really looking for it.'

'Will that fool the Betta?'

'Maybe, for a while.' Lola pauses. 'I don't see any other solution. I've *got* to go back in for Ali and I've got to record for Tais.'

I lay my hand on top of hers. 'Let me come with you.'

Lola shakes her head. 'I need you out here.'

'But how will I pull you out if they lock you off again?'

'You'll be hooked up to millions of connections this time. Just because we don't know who they are doesn't matter. Bring in the whole network and they *should* be able to flood any lock the Betta put on me.'

I gaze around the room. What have I gotten her into? I feel so guilty, man. But there's no time for stupid feelings now. Feelings ain't going to help any of us out of this mess. Steeling myself for her jump, I settle myself at the base of the bed.

'I'm ready when you are, Lola.'

She glances at the time. 'Any second now.'

We sit in the room in silence and then at 5 a.m. sharp my deck pulses, a stream of code flooding on to the screen.

'Punctual bastards, ain't they?'

Lola glances up, her mouth twisting into a smile. 'Punch me in, Anthony. And just make sure you catch everything, right? This is the meet we've been waiting for.'

I reach forward and hit the enter codes and then watch as Lola's body sinks on to the bed in front of me.

I turn, all my attention now on my deck. The feed swirls and twists until the visual input coalesces into recognisable form and the interior of a limousine comes into focus. The camera pans to the left and Kit is suddenly visible – one long, shapely leg crossed over her knee. She is older than last time; more of a woman now, and dressed in the Asiamodern style, the finely cut silk falling from her wrist as she indicates for the driver to take the next turn.

Lola turns; I catch a glimpse of her reflection in the car window – yet another Altform. This time she's all in black – rolling, dark, rockabilly curls, shades of deep blues and greens sweeping over her eyelids. She glances at Kit. 'Where are we?'

'On the Bermuda coast road, heading towards the complex.'

'Are you going to tell me the plan this time, or are you going to dump me into a fighting arena again?'

The corners of Kit's eyes crinkle up. 'I'm looking forward to meeting you in reality. If he likes you, that is.'

'Who?'

Kit purses her lips. 'You ask a lot of questions, girl. A word of advice. When you work for the Betta, best just to do without asking. It usually goes smoother that way.' She signals for the driver to slow down. 'Anyway, you'll find out soon enough.'

The car comes to a halt and the driver's side window drops a few centimetres as a pass is shown.

Kit smiles. 'Welcome to West Point. This is the Drop no one ever gets to see, where countries are made and broken.'

Through the narrow gap in the window I can just make out a military-style checkpoint and behind it a heavily fortified complex. In a few moments the limousine moves forward again and a series of floodlights burst into life, sweeping across the stone façade of an inner courtyard. Up high there's a flash of reflected light, possibly sniper lenses or maybe the sweep of lasers. My heart drops – this place is guarded like a prison camp.

The car comes to a stop and Kit jerks her head towards the entrance. 'This is as far as I go.'

'You're not coming? I thought you said it wouldn't be like last time.'

Kit's yellow cat-eyes flash a brief gold. 'It won't be.'

Lola's lens pans across the exterior of the building. 'How will I find my way?'

'If you can open the door, I'm sure the rest will be easy. Go now. He doesn't like to be kept waiting.'

Lola steps out of the limo, slamming the door behind her, and immediately the car moves away. As she heads for the entrance, I try to steady the grainy video feed – since entering the compound, streaks of static have started to eat into my visual. Peering forward, I am just able to see Lola climbing a bank of marble steps leading to a massive, barred set of doors – two great, carved slabs of ironwood, covered in intricate designs that snake along their central panels. Under cover of taking out a lock pick from her pocket, Lola punches out a message.

LOLA108: Door locked. Need sequence.

I push the message out into the Debtbelter network and seconds later my deck comes alive, humming with a barrage of commands as a thousand kids hit the lock combination with millions of recalibrations per second. Illuminated by a tower spotlight, Lola's fingers twist the pick in the lock, as she waits for the breakthrough. Her breathing calm, she keeps her movements slow and deliberate, only my deck readings show her true state, her adrenal glands pumping out a crazy stream of cortisol into her bloodstream – one million years of human history, screaming *Fight or Flight* at her. But Lola can't do either; she's got to stand there, acting perfectly calm, putting all her trust in a bunch of kids she doesn't even know. I don't know how she's doing it.

Suddenly there's a soft metallic click. The door locks smoothly slide open. The network has cracked the entrance code! Lola's long fingers come into view as she grips a heavy, elephant-headed door ring – one twist and the doors swing open, the heavy panels almost seeming to move forward with their own weight.

My screen darkens again as Lola steps into the hallway. I wait with fast-beating heart for her recording sensors to adjust to the new light. Gradually I can make out a hall, opening out into a wide foyer. Stacks of furniture are dotted around the room, draped in white sheets. Directly in front of her, a massive chandelier lies on its side, muffled in soft cloth. And as Lola moves forward through the foyer, the clutter only seems to increase; she's now passing racks of monitors balanced precariously on a row of wide, brass beds. What is this place? She reaches the end of the lobby and turns into a wide passageway, half blocked by a statue of a rearing horse. Using the statue as cover, Lola quickly punches through a new message.

LOLA108: This place is insane. Architecture plan?

Immediately I pass the message on to the network and after a few seconds pieces of the complex building start to form into 3D formations onscreen as kids hack into the Betta wall. I wait for the sections to come together so that I can wire them all through to Lola, but as I watch, their dimensions start to disintegrate – stairs are falling into halls and huge chambers fold down into tiny box rooms. I stare, bewildered, as a line of passageways start to link up to an expanding series of stairwells that climb up into space, only to dissolve into great collapsing curves over empty ballrooms. This is the Quantum Level all right. I mean, *nothing* makes any sense.

Lola suddenly lifts her head. Light is now flooding down the passageway, coming from a floor above. She heads towards it, reaching the foot of a wide staircase, where she hesitates, no doubt waiting for me to send her the architecture plans, but I guess she feels she'd better keep moving and slowly she starts to climb the winding stairs, at each turn encountering a new oil painting of some old ancestor, one pinch-mouthed man after another in a succession of powdered wigs and high collars.

At the top of the stairs Lola pauses again.

A voice cuts through the silence.

'Keep moving. First door on the left.'

I catch my breath. Is that *him*?

Her heart rate rising to 130, Lola heads towards the door. It is slightly ajar. She pushes inside. The space within is lit by only one point of light – a green banker's lamp tilted sideways that casts a narrow oval of light over a heavy, leather desk. A man sits behind it, his face in shadow.

Lifting his hand, he gestures for her to enter. I stare at my screen like I've never stared at anything in my life. I will him to speak again, so I can know if it's him for sure. Suddenly he leans forward into the light; he's a heavyset man with dark and inquisitive eyes in an intelligent face. He flashes a brief smile and then speaks, his voice rough like sandpaper.

'Welcome. I am so glad you were able to join me.'

I suck in a breath. It's him. *It's the man who left the*

message on Tais' voicemail! The sound is burnt right through me. But is he César Desai?

Lola moves towards him. He watches her carefully as she crosses the floorboards before lowering herself into a soft leather armchair opposite him.

She looks directly into his face. 'You are César Desai?'

His eyes spark in amusement. 'Please. I am who I am. I do not ask who you are in the real world and I give for you the same courtesy. It is who we are in *here*, in the Drop, that is important, yes?'

'If you say so.'

'I do.'

She leans forward in her chair. 'Kit sent me.'

The man steeples his fingers. 'Yes, you come highly recommended. Very . . . talented, she says. Many they have failed her test in Hong Kong and many, many more have tried to open my door but failed. Where did you learn such skills?'

'Picked them up here and there in the Debtbelt . . . plus I've had good teachers.'

He gives a bark of laughter. 'Why you think I search the belt? Hunger makes people good workers.'

'My friend Tais taught me a lot. You knew her, right?'

He moves on with a barely perceptible pause. 'So what name shall I call you by?'

'Anna Cortez.'

'*Cortez*. Brazilian?'

'Maybe. Maybe not.'

He shrugs. 'So, Miss Cortez, I believe you wish to work for me.'

'Yes.'

'You think you can function at my level? We aren't talking small-scale hacks now, we're in a whole new zone. Quantum. Big corporations, government level.'

'I can do it.'

He looks at her, a faint smile on his lips. 'I am sure you can. Even so, I need you to complete your first assignment as a trial. Agreed?'

'Yes.'

He leans forward, lacing his fingers together. 'Then listen. Krazner International, the owner of several luxury getaways, is exploring selling its fifty per cent stake in the Atlantis Resort to raise money to restructure a debt of $2.6 billion. The debt matures in a month's time. They are currently in talks with another company and we want to know what's going on behind the scenes.'

'How do you want me to do that?'

'You speak Portuguese and Spanish?'

'Yes.'

'Then we wish you to work on two main players. One

in Rio, the other in Mexico City.'

'You want me to infiltrate their Drop ID?'

'Yes.'

'I can do that . . .' Lola suddenly pauses. 'But I need to ask you a question first.'

He leans back in his seat. 'Go on.'

'Is this really just a test? I mean, what happens if I fail? We both know that Tais—'

César slams his hand on the desk. Despite herself, Lola jerks back. '*Tais, Tais.* Always speaking this name.' His mouth forms a cruel line. 'Enough of this. Why don't you tell me what you're really here for?'

Lola's voice falters a little. 'What do you mean?'

'You know very well.'

At that moment, a high, ultrasonic whine cuts through my audio feed, instantly wiping out Lola's signal and the entire Debtbelt connection – and suddenly she and César reappear onscreen but filmed from another angle. What's happening? I watch, amazed, as Lola's eyes widen, as they fix on the muzzle of a black automatic pistol in César's hand. I lurch forward, striking the decompression key, but even as my finger hits my deck, I know I'm too late. I've lost her!

The man smiles at Lola. 'You didn't think you could fool us so easy did you?' He waves his gun nonchalantly.

244

'But you can finish your little play if you want. You ask your stupid questions about Tais and I tell you it was me who ordered her killed. And then you get me to say my name, to identify myself – César Desai – and you get your evidence to take to the feds. I mean, come on, girl. You think we don't know you've got a lens? That network connection you set up is very pretty and it might fool a Drop businessman, but it would never fool us.'

Lola sits, silent.

'And if you are waiting to be pulled out, I'm afraid that plan is finished too. We've killed your feed for *good*. It's just you and me now.'

César pauses. 'Well no, that's not strictly true.' He twists his head. 'Come.'

Lola barely looks up as Ali crosses the room, coming to a halt beside her chair.

César sighs. 'Sorry, Lola. I gave him the choice. Him or you.'

And then Ali bends over Lola, his fingers filling the screen as he searches for her micro lens. Locating it in the neckline of her dress, he pauses and stares directly into the camera lens.

'Sorry brother, end of the road. Nobody crosses the Betta and lives.'

He rips out her lens and my screen goes black.

Lola jerks, her head rising in one sharp spasm before she slumps again, unconscious, on the bed. I stare at her in agony. What has Ali done to her? I fall to my knees. How could he betray her like that? For a moment I can't move, I can't act, I'm literally paralysed with rage. From somewhere in the house a phone starts to ring and I squeeze my eyes shut, blocking the sound out. I can't stay like this, I've got to focus, work out what to do and *fast*.

Snatching up my deck, my fingers touch a hot slick of acid across the rear panel. Flipping it over, I see a silver-black stain spreading over the metal. That means only one thing; a core meltdown. The deck is dead.

I raise my eyes to the bed once more, to where Lola lies, her arm still resting on Ali's chest. Ali! My blood boils inside my chest. I move to his side. At least he won't get away from *me*.

Suddenly there's a loud knock at my bedroom door.

'Anthony!'

Stella. I block her out as I reach for Ali's throat.

She bangs again.

My fingers tighten around his flesh.

'Anthony! Open the door, now!'

I curse. Stupid girl. Why won't she go away?

'Later!' I scream

'It's a phone call for you. He says it's urgent.'

I stare wildly at the door. 'Who says?'

'The Teller.'

Releasing my grip, I cross the room in one bound, flinging the bedroom door open. Stella stands in the hallway, holding the speaker-phone out towards me.

I bellow into the mic, 'I've lost Lola!'

The Teller's voice is shaking. 'I know. The Betta have her surrounded.'

'You've got to help me.'

'Can you access another deck?'

My eyes meet Stella's. She nods.

'Yeah.'

'Then do it and I'll punch a hole into their wall. You'll have to pull her out from *inside*.'

247

'I can do that?'

'Yes, I'm going to rip a hole out for you, but I can only give you a few minutes. I don't have the resources to keep it open for any longer. Now move!'

Disconnecting the phone, I turn to Stella. 'Will you help me? I've got to go back into the Drop.'

Her face is white like chalk. 'Are you in trouble?'

'Not me, it's Lola. She's trapped.'

'Where?'

'In Bermuda.'

Stella stares at me, eyes wide. 'In the *Quantum* Drop?'

'Yes. I've got no time to explain. But – will you . . . watch over me . . . while I'm inside?'

Without another word she turns and runs into her room, returning in seconds to slap her deck into my hands. Taking her by the wrist, I drag her over to the bed where Ali and Lola lie and, pulling on my visor, I lay myself down on the floor.

'You know how to work the decompression key, right?'

'Yes.'

'But only pull me out if there's literally no other choice. D'you understand? You do nothing until it's either pull me out or I die.' I hold her eye. 'I – I don't want to scare you, Stel, but that's what you've got to do.'

Her eyes cloud with fear.

'Can you do this? It's not just for me, it's for Lola . . . and Tais, too.'

Stella straightens. 'Yes, I can.'

And then her deck lights up with an incoming message.

TELLER: *Ready?*

I stare at my sister, at the freckles swirling across her nose.

She blows out her cheeks, smiles. 'Let's do it.'

Reaching forward, I hit *re>message*.

AGRIFFIN: *Ready*.

The Teller's stream of code hits my deck and I steel myself for the jerk into the deep. Once the sequence is complete, Stella's eyes lock with mine.

'Drop me,' I say and then I fall back on the rug, my mind bending into the void.

Weaving through a grove of palm trees, I race across cool wet sand, surf crashing onshore on my left. The Bermuda complex, West Point, is dead ahead, maybe five hundred metres away – but it's not the same as it was before. It's all twisted somehow, kind of like it's been mashed up with a bunch of other buildings, with great grey slabs of concrete jutting up over the south side and gun turrets poking out of the rubble under the thickly starred night. But they're not aimed at me. In fact, there aren't any guards around at all, the place seems kind of deserted. Reaching the compound barriers, I hurdle the gates and, landing in the enclosed courtyard, I set off towards the entrance, following in Lola's footsteps.

I clamber up the marble steps and when I reach the top, I pause for a second to check for Betta. But there's nothing to see, the surrounding buildings are lit only by points of flickering light set into huge gaps of black night. And so I turn, passing the still-open heavy doors into the building.

Inside, I halt again. Which way now? I look around me, but I hardly recognise the place. It's totally different from when Lola was here, like it's all been reconfigured. How am I going to find her now? And then it comes to me, *I can't*. The only way I'm going to get to Lola is to force César to come out and find *me*. I cup my hands around my mouth.

'César!'

My voice sounds so thin in my ears. A puny kid's voice. A wave of fury flashes through me at my own weakness.

'César Desai!'

My voice bounces off the high, vaulted ceiling. Followed by silence. A light flicks on and off on a high balcony.

'Murderer!'

More silence. But this time it's deeper. Something has changed. I can feel the *listening*. I am not alone any more. Standing in the dark hallway, my blood thundering in my chest, I throw out my arms, jerking my spine back.

'Killer! It was you killed Tais. You!'

Silence, more silence. And then I hear running feet, a grunt – and the next thing I know they're on me. I'm slammed to the ground; a studded boot connecting with my elbow. Pain explodes through my body. I roll over in agony, but somehow I manage to break free, scrabbling to my knees again.

'You don't scare me!' I scream.

A voice comes from above.

'Silence him.'

And then all I know is kicks and punches. I think there are only two guards, but their fists are like a machine beating down on me. I try to fight, to hit back. I swing out my arms but it's too dark to see and my hands connect with nothing. And then suddenly a deep subsonic boom rocks the building. For a second it feels as if every last atom of air is being sucked out of the place before we're hit by a battering ram of returning air, a barrage that flattens everything in its path.

For a second I lie still, my body twisted around a column at the foot of a wide staircase. Was that a bomb? I don't know if it was meant for me or if the Teller has punched another hole in the Betta wall. But either way it's given me a few seconds' head start.

I drag myself to my feet and, silently as I can, I start to climb the rough concrete stairs towards the balcony. As I run, I catch glimpses of familiar things, paintings, ornaments . . . stuff that I saw through Lola's feed. I glance over my shoulder. Nobody is following me, not yet at least. It's like I'm invisible – it's too *mad* what I'm doing – the little runt running towards danger, towards César Desai.

Grabbing the banister railing, I use it to swing my body up, turn after turn. I pass the fifth, sixth, seventh floor – and as I complete the last turn the filthy concrete steps beneath my feet suddenly reform into smooth carpet and the building transforms into the luxury complex again. At the top of the stairs I stop, my heart beating fast. I know this place, this is where Lola stood before! Charging towards the first door on the left, I ram it open with my shoulder . . . and the boy who runs into the room ain't me no more. I am a wolf, a warrior, a boy who cannot be killed by bullets!

'César!' I shout.

In the gloom I can just make him out. He's standing by the window, looking down on to the dimly-lit courtyard below. As I enter, he whips around. Crossing the space in three bounds, I jump on top of him, smacking and punching and cuffing his face like a madman. And then I reach back, throwing all my strength into a punch, aiming to split his head open wide. But I don't connect, my fist kind of slides off the side of his chin. I don't remember what happens next, not clear. All I know is somehow he turns and throws his weight back against the wall, slamming all the air out of my body as his body crashes down on top of mine.

I open my eyes. I'm lying on the floorboards. Stella's face flashes into my mind. I silently plead with her to wait, not to pull me out. Not yet. My head rolls to the side. César stands over me, gun in hand, his breath coming hard. Is he going to kill me now? But to my surprise he holsters his pistol and kneels down, planting all his weight on my chest before grabbing my wrists and pinning them to the floor. I struggle like a maniac. I'd give my life itself to get an arm free and swing at him again, but he's too strong for me. In my rage I spit into his face. Then César punches me in the gut, knocking all the wind out of me, and finally I can't do nothing but lie still.

Still holding me pressed to the floor, he stares into my face, his eyes curious.

'So this is him, eh?'

'Yes, sir.'

I twist my head around, furious, but César shakes his head.

'No, don't you be moving again. This is just you and me, having a little chat. Man to man.' He sighs. 'All this trouble you make for me. Incredible. And now I'm going to have to kill you too. As well as her.'

He jerks his head. My eyes follow the direction. Lola's limp body lies sprawled under the table, just out of reach.

'Kill a couple of kids just because you couldn't let it be. You think I want this?' he continues.

My eyes blaze. 'Don't tell me it's just business. Me, Lola, Tais. All in a day's work, right?'

His eyes harden. 'You want it to be simple but it is not so. Ah, *street* level, for sure – you show some muscle, you rule the street. But here, at my level, a man like me has got to be more strategic. I play or I get played.'

'And killing is part of that?'

'Enough. You ask too many dumb questions, Anthony. There is no wire any more, no lens, no police rescue. No nothing.'

I stare directly into his eyes. 'So, how much?'

He cocks his head.

'What?'

'How much is enough?'

'How much what?'

'Money.'

He rolls his eyes. 'It's not like that. It's not about the numbers; it's the game. And it *is* a game, you know? Somebody wins, somebody loses. Money itself isn't lost or made, it's simply *transferred*.'

'But I don't care about the money. I care about her.'

César continues, as if he hasn't heard me. 'And so one day you stick your card in the wall and nothing comes out. Because your country is bankrupt. And who did it? Us. The smart ones, who saw a gap in the market and went after it. Like evolution . . . the strong ones.' He slightly relaxes his grip on my wrists. 'If I get up do you promise not to move?'

I nod and, slowly, he levers himself off me. It feels like a truck lifting off my chest.

I roll on to my side, drag in a breath. 'So you're saying it's our fault. You destroy people's lives, but you're only doing what's natural?'

'I didn't make the world the selfish place it is.'

'That's the way *you* see it. But not everyone's like you.'

César shrugs. 'Yes but everyone *wants* to be me. They just haven't got the guts to do it.'

'I don't.'

César sighs. 'Yes, you do.'

'And Tais?'

He looks me full in the face.

'She knew what she was doing when she disrespected me. The deal she was working on was secret. And her going outside, to that journalist . . . well, that may not mean anything to you, but out here if there's no respect there's no nothing, nothing to catch you if you fall. I *had* to finish her.'

Slowly I pull myself to my knees, my mind reeling. A journalist? That must mean the Teller is a journalist for sure and she went to him to break the company takeover story. An image of all the ruined lives rises up before me, all the jobs gone, all the misery the Betta brought down on us, all the pain she went through. I turn to face César.

'Fight me.'

He smiles. 'Ali told me you were a special one. But before your head gets too big I have to tell you a little secret, Anthony. I've only let you come so far in the hope your journalist friend would follow you. The Teller you call him, right? You're just *bait* to me, boy, but it seems he isn't coming, hey?'

I clench my fingers into a fist. 'So then, what are you scared of? Fight me.'

He frowns. 'Don't be stupid.'

'You're scared, aren't you?'

'Didn't you hear what I just told you? You need to be quiet now.'

'Make me.'

'This conversation is now over.' César's face hardens into a cold mask.

'How's it feel to order a girl to be kicked to death . . . ?'

He suddenly straightens, passes his pistol to Ali.

'I'm done talking. The journalist isn't coming. Kill him. And the girl. Now.'

Ali takes the weapon, turns the barrel towards me.

I look into his eyes. 'Lola isn't dead yet?'

He shakes his head. 'Nah. Thought we'd do you both together.'

Despite his words, the gun muzzle he levels at me is shaking.

I swallow. 'You can't kill her. She came back in for you.'

Ali's fingers tighten around the trigger.

'You still don't know who I am, do you, Anthony? You din't really think I'd come round next morning after Sapphire's with my mind all changed an' shit . . . all suddenly on your side, wanting to fight the bad guys, did you? You watch too many of them thrillers where it all turns out good in the end.'

César pats him on the shoulder.

'Betta for life, right, Ali.'

Ali nods.

I glance from Ali's face to César's. I watch as my friend's eyes darken, as he leans forward, pressing the gun to my temple, and then I watch as his arm suddenly jerks sideways, a blur of movement, just before the bullet leaves the chamber.

Half-deaf from the explosion, I twist my head and stare, for a long moment, stunned – at César, standing motionless – the bullet hole in his forehead forming a perfect circle. And then I watch as he slowly, almost gracefully, takes a couple of steps to the side, until he collapses, his body slamming down on to the marble floor with a crash.

Ali shakes his head, sighs.

'Kids today. Got no loyalty, ai'ght?'

And then immediately he spins round and crosses over to Lola, his face full of fear as his fingers explore her damaged skull.

'Jeez. I hit her pretty hard. I reckoned he was really gonna kill her right there and then, and so I knocked her out till you came. You right to help me lift her?'

I nod dumbly into his face. '– Ali?'

He chops the air. 'No time. Later.'

'But—'

Ali reaches for her arms. '*Later*, man. Won't be but a matter of minutes 'fore the Betta come crawling over this place like flies.'

I take Lola's head in my hands and suddenly her
eyes open.

I gasp. 'Are you OK?'

'No, this bastard knocked me out.'

Ali snatches up her hand. 'I had to. Buy time . . .'

Lola's eyes start to roll back once more.

'Ali, she's losing it again.'

He turns to me, urgent. 'How did you get here?'

'Teller cut a hole in the Betta wall. It's down on
the beach.'

'How long he give you?'

'Twenty minutes.' I glance at the clock on the wall.
'We've got nine left.'

'Then let's get her down there, we can jump back

through the hole with you. César cut her connection for good – she *can't* decompress.'

'What about you?'

'The same. It's only you with a live link.'

Grasping Lola by the arms, Ali starts to swing her upright – and then suddenly there's a dull roar, and a flash of light from the doorway. He staggers backwards, fumbling at his shoulder.

Kit steps into the room, her gun raised.

'Going somewhere, traitor?'

She trains her weapon on him, but before she can get a clear shot, I hurl myself at her, my outstretched arm knocking her hand sideways as she fires the gun. The bullet goes wide, missing Ali by a fraction of a centimetre, I smash into the wall behind her. Kit pivots on her heel, the tendons in her wrist writhing as she snaps her gun up to shoot again.

Ripping myself clear of the wall I lunge desperately at her, catching her in the chest with the heel of my boot. She falls backwards against the door and reaching down I seize her head in my hands and smash it down repeatedly against the marble floor until her eyes glaze over.

I whirl around to face Ali, my breath coming in great gulps.

'You hit?'

'Don't matter.'

Staggering upright, he reaches for Lola and then doubles up with a cry of pain.

I spring forward. 'Let me see!'

'No.'

'Shut up, Ali.' I place my hands on his shoulder, bite down vomit when my fingers touch the separated bones, the oozing blood.

'Shit. I'll never be able to get her down to the beach on time by myself.'

'What then?'

I stare about the room, my mind reeling. 'Reckon you can still run OK?'

'Yeah.'

'Then let's send Lola back, now.'

'How?'

'If I stick my visor and 'trodes on her the deck sensors will go crazy. Stella will think I'm dying and she'll pull me out, 'cept it won't be me, it'll be Lola.'

He stares into my face. 'But then *you'll* be trapped.'

'Not if we can make the rip in time.'

Ali clenches his fist. 'Ai'ght. Hurry.'

Ripping the visor off my face I fix the 'trodes on Lola's temples and for a long moment I stare down at her, praying for Stella to pull her out. I can't bear to think what

I'm doing to my little sister. What is she seeing right now, up in my room? My face turning blue? My heart monitor falling silent . . . ? I ball my hands. *Do it Stella, pull me out!* Seconds tick by.

'C'mon!' Ali mutters.

I stare into Lola's face, scream, 'Stella, c'mon . . . For me!'

And then suddenly Lola's body twitches, disappears. Stella's decompressed her.

I whirl around. 'Four minutes fifty! Run!'

And together we turn, heading for the hallway, running for our lives.

As we reach the top of the stairs, another explosion rocks the complex and a great crack opens up below us. Ali is thrown backwards as a chunk of another huge structure, a steel shaft, slams through the building's fabric. Hauling him up by his good arm, I start to drag him down the steps, practically throwing him across the metre-wide gap that has opened up.

And then we race down together, clinging on to the railing for support on the wildly tilting staircase – but when we reach the second floor the building tilts violently, sending us flying off the edge of the steps – and for a few terrible moments we hang, dangling off the banister above a seven-metre drop. Ali starts to scream with pain.

Desperately grabbing him by the waist, I try to take some of his weight, but he's starting to slip, slowly but inexorably, through my arms. I can't hold him any longer. I make one last, desperate clutch at his jacket – and then suddenly the room flips upright again, sending us both hurtling down the last flight of steps on to the floor.

I yank Ali to his feet and we stagger to the doors. I peer out to check for snipers, but what I see is half the courtyard gone, the far wall a pile of smoking rubble. Shoving my arm under his armpit, I force him on at a run along the dark road towards the rip. I reckon about two and a half minutes is all we've got left.

As we reach the sandy strip that signals the start of the beach, I look up and jerk to a halt. On the horizon a city skyline now juts into the sky, weirdly backlit against the dark night. I stare in astonishment. What city is that? Jags of famous towers, curves of stadiums, half-demolished ruins of places now long forgotten are mashed up in the sprawl. Shades of Athens and Baltimore and Berlin and Buenos Aires and Detroit and Helsinki and Istanbul and Lisbon and Mexico City and Mumbai and Nairobi and Santiago and São Paulo and Shanghai and Stockholm and Tel Aviv and Tokyo and Toronto and Washington all merged into one.

'Oh, God.'

Ali jerks my sleeve, points off to the left. I turn. My heart plummets – I stare at where the Teller's rip used to be. Except it's not just a rip any more. It's grown into a massive, raging whirlpool that circles near the ocean shore, sucking in water in a swirling vortex of insane energy.

Ali sinks to his knees. 'I can't.'

'Come on!' I shout.

'Come on, what? No way, Anthony.'

'We've got to.'

'*You've* got to, you mean.'

'No. Both of us.'

'We ain't gonna make that.'

'Don't know till we try.'

Ali kneads the flesh of his broken, bleeding arm.

'So my stash, Anthony . . .'

'What?' I bend down to catch his words in the wind.

'My stash. It's down by the electricity substation at the back of the Estate.'

'Why you telling me this now?'

'Four bricks down and three across. All my money . . .'

I grab his collar. 'Shut up!'

He shakes his head. 'Promise you'll take it.'

'You're such a coward.'

His eyes blaze. 'I ain't no coward.'

'Then prove it.'

He turns his eyes to the shoreline. 'Man, we done some mad things . . .'

I stick my hand out. 'Yeah, and this is one more. *Now, Ali!*'

A grin flashes across his face then, reaching up, he grabs my hand and hauls himself to his feet.

Wrapping my arm around his shoulder I start to drag him forward and, side by side, we run for the centre of the raging energy core. But as soon as we hit the inner walls we're battered to our knees and, for what feels like an age, I'm pinned to the ground, staring up at the countless iridescent layers that melt and surge overhead. Massive, they rise, reach an impossible peak then start to fall again, plunging towards us at terrible speed. If we don't move now we're finished. Rolling on to my hands and knees, straining against the unbelievable force, I reach for Ali and drag him forward with me. And then, in the dying seconds of the vortex, as the great wave crashes over us, we plunge into the heart of the Drop, the water breaking and foaming over our bodies as we fall.

Something breaks free inside my head. I am floating in perfectly clear water. Calm. Blue. Peaceful. I twist my head upward. Above me, the water's surface is covered with an ugly proliferation of urban structures, bound together by ultra-fast trades and transactions, their digital wake creating trace lines across the sky. A blur of demand and counter demand, an endless sprawl, a web of complexity built to numb the mind. I stare at it in wonder. What a species we are!

And then suddenly I am dropping once more, hurtling down towards a deep, dark, blue canyon . . . And as I near it, an arm of shadow uncoils from the seabed, a seething mass of indigo, dark violet verging on black, sucking me down at terrible speed as the rip whips itself backwards through the Drop. The urban lights on the surface flicker and die as it spreads outward at terrifying speed, blotting out the Bermuda complex and swallowing up the city structures, folding them in on themselves in a slide of utter destruction.

'Anthony?'

I open my eyes. Stella bends over me, her pupils dilated with fear.

'Say something, *please*,' she whispers.

'*Stel?*'

Her face sags with relief.

I try to lift my head. 'How long have I been back?'

'Five minutes.'

'The others?'

Stella motions towards the bed.

I struggle upright. Ali is stretched out on the mattress and Lola is bent over him, cradling his head in her hands as she stares into his face. And then I see that he is conscious too, and that he is looking up at her, his eyes wide with longing.

'Guys. Are you OK?'

Lola turns her head. 'Yeah, you geek.' She turns back to Ali, but it's as if my words have broken a spell because at that moment he rolls away from Lola and, steadying himself on the bed for a moment, swings his feet on to the floor.

'It's time to go.'

Lola frowns. 'What d'you mean?'

He winces, gingerly touching his shoulder. 'After what just went down, Betta are gonna want answers. In no time they'll be crawling all over the area looking for me.'

'So? We'll hide you.'

'Betta ain't no feds. When they ask they *get* answers . . . and if they find me they'll find you. And kill you.'

Lola slowly shakes her head. 'No.'

Ali takes her hand. '*Yes*. Right now the only Betta who can link you to me are dead or trapped inside the Drop. We've got to keep it that way.'

I take a step towards him. 'But you're hurt! You've

been under for so long and they cut you and shot—'

'I know a place to go. Be all right as long as I get there soon. Honest.'

'There's no way I'm letting you go alone.'

He holds my eye. 'You know I'm right. Come on, I ain't got the strength to fight you as well. You patched my belly up and a broken arm ain't gonna kill me.'

Ali slowly rises to his feet, looks at us. Lola, me, Stella. He stares at each of us in turn as if he's storing us, deep inside. Finally he turns to me.

'You did good, Anthony.'

A choke, a wave, a hammer thud hits me hard across my chest. But he don't want that from me. He wants me to let him go with style. So I push, I will, I force the choke of bitter tears, the rage, down and I stare at the burnt-out deck lying on the bedroom floor till I can trust myself to speak, and then I look up and smile.

'So did you.'

Ali's face splits into a grin. He reaches for his jacket, slides it gently on to his shoulders. 'Stella, you look after him for me, ai'ght?'

Tears cloud her clear eyes. 'I will.'

Ali holds out his hand to Lola. 'Friends now?'

Lola flings her arms around his neck, tears streaming down her face. 'No!'

He holds her, tight. 'C'mon, now.'

For a long moment they clutch each other, as if nothing could ever pull them apart. And then Ali pulls back.

'See you 'round.'

Lola shakes her head. 'When?'

He shrugs. 'Don't know. When all this is over.' He laughs, suddenly. 'Debtbelt can't last for ever, ai'ght? Got to be a way out of this madness.'

After the door shuts, I stare at the wall, listening to his descending footsteps on the stairs. And after I hear the front door slam shut I drop my bruised head against my knee and I don't mind telling you I weep. For all of it. For the whole stupid mess because all the good and all the beautiful it gets trashed, yeah, and the bad just rolls on and on.

And Tais, we buried her a year ago today. Her heart quit
on her on her eighteenth birthday and we buried her on
Midsummer's Day, y'know when the sun he's at his
strongest, sending down his most powerful rays on Tais,
his beautiful girl. That's how Grandad put it, anyhow.
He's gone all poetical in his old age, says if he's going to
be covered in soup slops he's going to say what he damn
well pleases.

It's taken me a long time, a lot of painful months, but
slowly I've come to realise I'm not supposed to know all
the answers. No one ever knows them all. That's how life
is. That's just the way it flows, right? For a long time I
believed nobody cared about Tais except me, but I was
wrong and I went into such a dark place because of it. But

Ali and Lola and Stella, they pulled me through. And all the crazy things I did, I should be dead by rights. But I'm not, and I reckon I was given a gift. It's like I got a wire reconnected somehow and I've come out the other side and I'm me again, *Anthony*.

And so I'm standing here by Tais' grave, for the first time. It's a big day, I guess. Lola waits, silent, by my side – and over on the far end of the lawn, Stella and Grandad and the dog are sitting on a bench in a pool of sunshine and Shane is barking at his own shadow. The passing year ain't brought that mutt any more wisdom, believe.

Finally I turn to Lola.

'Got my first exam next Tuesday.'

She lifts an eyebrow. 'You ready?'

I shrug. 'Guess I'll find out Tuesday.' I nudge her. 'Hey, did I tell you I got fired from that pizza place last week?'

'No. How come?'

'My elbow.'

'What . . . ?'

'Yeah, it happened last week. We were in Ian the manager's office, like maybe twelve of us. It was a meeting to set targets, smelly-sock pizza targets. I mean, *madness*.'

Lola narrows her eyes. '*Right* . . .'

'And there wasn't enough space in there and so people

were kind of perched on desks, sharing chairs, all squished up, but Ian din't care, he just kept droning on about shaving off seconds on delivery times, and then suddenly out of nowhere someone switched the light off.'

'Who?'

I hold out a finger. 'I'm getting to that. Soon as it happened, everyone started giggling and shoving and squirming around in the dark and pretending they couldn't find the socket even though Ian was bellowing at us to switch it back on, till finally he really lost it, and he screamed, "Right, that's it. Whoever just elbowed me in the face, you're fired" . . .'

Lola rolls her eyes. 'But why din't you move?'

'I ain't finished yet. Straight after he shouted this, someone put on a fake voice and said, "Whoever did it, move away from Ian, quick, so he won't know it's you when the light comes back on." And then of course there was another big scuffle and then suddenly the light flicks on and guess who's pressed right up against his ugly mug?'

'You, you geek. So what happened?'

'He said, "Everybody back to work – except you, Anthony. You're fired."'

Lola bursts out laughing. 'Unbelievable!'

I grin. 'Right.'

She puts her hand in mine, sighs. 'Man, I *miss* them.'

'I talk to her the whole time.'

'Do you?'

I glance at the wildflowers twining around Tais' gravestone. 'Yeah. That story was for her, not you.'

Lola tightens her grip on my hand. 'I thought I saw him just this morning. I was getting off the bus and – I don't know, I felt as if someone was watching me and so I turned, fast –'

'– And?'

'Empty street. I mean, *of course* he wasn't there.'

I shake my head. 'I reckon Ali, he's way out in front. Somewhere good.'

A tear trickles down Lola's cheek. 'I hope so.'

'C'mon. Want to go to the 333 Café for old time's sake . . . order up the Special?'

'You buying?'

I tap my back pocket. 'Totally. Severance pay burning a hole in my wallet.'

Lola bursts out laughing. 'You are such a jerk.'

'So?'

I turn to see Stella running across the grass towards us. My heart tightens. My little sister, man, she's brilliant. She's twelve now, and she's getting better every day, but pretty soon she's going to have to learn to hide the crows

274

and the lists and the drawings and *work it out* if she's going to survive out here with the normal ones. But I don't want her to work it out. I mean, I want her to be happy and all, but I want her to be *her*. What's so great about normality anyhow? We're all just a bunch of weirdos, right?

'Anthony?'

I blink.

'What?'

Stella is staring at me intently.

'So do you?'

'Do I what?'

'Believe there's a parallel world just below the surface of ours, with a different reality?'

I blow out my cheeks. 'Jeez, Stel, how do I know?'

'Yes, but do you?'

I frown. 'Do you mean like in quantum physics, with other dimensions . . . or d'you mean monsters and that?'

She itches her nose. 'Not monsters. But another dimension, maybe. One that we can't see or be in?'

'Like when you go to the edge of the ocean and it's another world inside, totally alien?'

'I've never been to the ocean.'

I smile. 'Maybe it's about *wanting* to see. Maybe if we *really believed*, we could see the world in a whole new way, right here and now.'

A harsh call cuts through the air and Stella glances upward, her face softening with a smile.

'There's White Tip.'

Following her gaze, I peer up into the sky, watching the crow as she hovers above us.

'How do you know it's her?'

Stella looks at me scornfully. 'Because she's got white tips on her wings. Honestly Anthony, you're as blind as a bat.'

And so, taking my sister's hands, Lola and I make our way over to Grandad, and when we reach the bench, I turn one last time and look across the smooth grass, to where Tais lies. And as I watch, a late afternoon shaft of sunlight streaks along the green towards me – and when it touches the ground I stand upon – it feels like a bolt of electricity passing through my body.

And right there and then I make a vow to live more like how Stella says. I'm going to wind up the universe with ceremony each day and live it to the last drop. And I'm going to open my eyes and really *see* like she does. And I'll be a man and a whale and a dog and a deer and a crow and all the others. People were animals too, back in the day, and I reckon when we started to fall in love with our own crazy minds we gave a lot up, a lot of brilliance, a lot of beauty, a lot of dignity, a lot of real love. I don't reckon in the past we'd have ever left a precious thing like Tais or Ali behind to rot.

But that's not how I want to live. Me, I'm going the other way. I'm turning back to the wild. Yeah, you'd better believe I am. I am the boy who turned wolf.

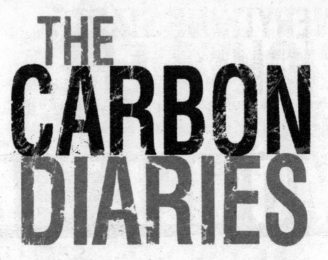
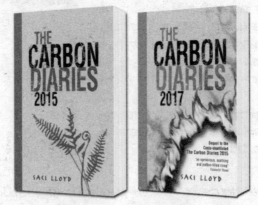
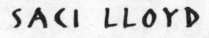

EVERYTHING STARTS RIGHT HERE RIGHT NOW

MOMENTUM

SACI LLOYD

London, the near future. Energy wars are flaring across the globe - oil prices have gone crazy, regular power cuts are a daily occurrence. The cruel Kossak soldiers prowl the streets, keeping the Outsiders - the poor, the disenfranchised - in check. Hunter is a Citizen: one of the privileged of society, but with his passion for free running and his rebel friend Leo he cannot help but be fascinated by the Outsiders. So when he meets Outsider Uma, he is quickly drawn into their world - and into an electrifying and dangerous race to protect everything they hold dear.

A hugely exciting dystopian thriller from the immensely talented Costa-shortlisted author of The Carbon Diaries, Saci Lloyd.

'From its breathtaking opening ... an action-packed thriller with a warm heart' – The Guardian

www.hodderchildrens.co.uk

Hodder Children's Books

THE OBSIDIAN MIRROR

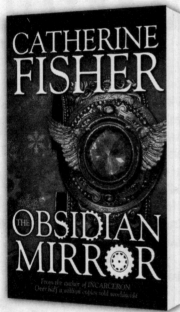

Jake's father disappears while working on mysterious experiments with the obsessive, reclusive Oberon Venn – and Jake is convinced that Venn has murdered him. Only the dark and dangerous power of the Obsidian Mirror can expose the truth...

Time travel and the faery world collide in the first book in a stunning new sequence from the bestselling author of *INCARCERON*.

PRAISE FOR *INCARCERON*:

'Stands out above all others. Its imaginative scale and gobsmacking finale make it one of the best fantasy novels written for a long time.'
– Amanda Craig, The Times

Also available as an ebook

www.catherine-fisher.com
www.hodderchildrens.co.uk

Hodder Children's Books